Somewhere in Between

a novel by
shirl rickman

Somewhere in Between \ Shirl Rickman – 1st ed.
Library of Congress Cataloging-in-Publication Data
ISBN-13: 978-1532913884 | ISBN-10: 1532913885

You are the poem
I never knew how to write,
and this life is the story
I always wanted to tell.

–Tyler Knott Gregson

April 26, 2003

This is strange, but here it goes. My mom gave me this journal today for my sixteenth birthday. A freaking journal. I told her sixteen-year-old boys don't write in journals. She told me to break the mold. So I'm breaking the mold. In fact, I'm going beyond that because this journal is dedicated to love. And Sara.

I fell in love today. I fell deeply, madly in love with Sara. I'm going to make sure she knows it every day for as long as I live. My friends would give me shit if they ever found out about this journal, let alone my feelings, but I don't care. She's the most beautiful girl I've ever seen, and I will make her mine.

CHAPTER I

TESSA

ALTHOUGH I WOULD GUESS THE man standing before me isn't any older than thirty-four, his worn out eyes make him appear more advanced in years. I give him a once-over—there's a moldy smell emanating from him. My heart breaks when I ask his name.

"Can you tell me your name?" The smile never leaves my face.

"Lawrence, but you can call me, Larry," he replies as he wipes his dirt-covered hands down the front of his shirt. I imagine if grime weren't already covering him, there would be visible smudges streaked down his front.

He reaches his hand out for me to take. Any other person might hesitate. I see beyond the filth that covers their skin and clothes. I look into their eyes and recognize the person they once were and are hoping to be again. Larry isn't any different. Larry is every person who walks through our doors searching for help.

As I grasp his hand in mine, I widen my smile. "Well, Larry, it's a pleasure to meet you. My name is Tessa." He grins back. "Tell me a little about yourself and what brings you to us today."

Larry leans back in his seat and proceeds to share his story with only a little hesitation. The look in his eyes lets me know he has waited a long time for someone to ask him about the person he is inside beyond what a person sees on the outside.

Larry, like all the others who walk through our doors, had an average life once. He held a job. Had a family. Larry never thought he would be in this position. He was educated and funny. I listen as he tells me about his many suits and how his tie always matched. We laugh.

Our eyes meet. Larry just wants someone to listen. I can see the confident man he once was as he talks and talks.

Then, he tells me of his parents' death. He says since he was an only child, he had no one else. He was let go from his job when the economy took a blow. Slowly, he lost everything, especially once he turned to drugs.

He is clean now, though. He attends weekly meetings, but he just hasn't had any luck securing a job. Larry doesn't look at me when he's finished telling his story. He just stops talking. The light that began to burn while he recalled his life dims. I reach across the desk and cover his hand with mine before giving it a slight squeeze.

As I jot down my last note, we both rise to our feet.

"Larry, welcome to Hands of Hope. I promise we will do everything to guide you through a course of action, allowing you to achieve what you're hoping for." I reassure him, a broad smile on my face.

His smile grows wide. It reaches so high that small crinkles form around his eyes. Happiness. Hope. He is a reflection of those things. I send Larry in the direction of our hygiene area and pick up my belongings before heading to my office.

Closing the door behind me, I flop back into my chair and let out a long sigh. It's Saturday morning. I've been here every day this week, and I'm exhausted. Exhausted, but happy. This week alone, we've helped five people get off the street and find jobs. Soon they will have their homes and their lives again. With my eyes closed, I allow myself to relax and imagine where these new opportunities will lead them.

The loud ringing of my phone startles me from my thoughts. I slowly open my eyes, clearing my throat before answering the phone.

"Tessa Collins, how may I help you?"

I move my mouth away from the receiver as I release a yawn.

"Tessa Marie Collins! Have you even left that place once this week?" My mother's voice echoes through the phone.

Rolling my eyes, I lean back in my chair while holding the phone away from my ear. My mom always has the best of intentions, especially when she tries to help with her overprotective need to nag me. Both of my parents have always been supportive of my ambitions to make the world a better place. Of course, the world is an enormous undertaking, so I settle on helping a place within my immediate reach…my hometown. Although it's the capital of one of the largest states in the country, it still has a way to go before it matches the enormity of its name. Known around the world as a music haven, Austin, Texas has intrigued people and brought them to our city in droves. More people and more homeless.

This is where I come in. After graduating from the University of Texas, I took my philanthropic efforts to the streets of our city. I took my first job here at Hands of Hope and hadn't looked back since. I brought new ideas and ways to get what the homeless and less fortunate need to get back on their feet and back into a productive life. I love what I do. I feel complete in every way. Almost.

"Tessa…are you there or did you fall asleep?"

"Yes, Mo. I'm here." I answer her. I've always called my mom Mo. It's just one of our things. "And, yes. I've been here all week, but it has been worth every second. We placed three women and two men in new jobs. So, you see? All worth it."

"Oh, Tessa." She pauses. "That is just great, but honey, please take care of yourself. You can do amazing things even with breaks in between. Plus, you deserve "me" time…if you know what I mean."

3

Yes, I know what she means. My parents have always allowed me to live my life. They never push me, but occasionally Mo conveys her opinion on my inability to be, as she puts it, social. She doesn't think I need a man to be happy, but she says I am too young not to have a little fun. My parents are unique, to say the least, and I love it. They're also very much in love. It's almost sick, but even I can admit it's sweet. I just don't believe that kind of love exists for everyone.

I laugh. "Mo, I know what you mean exactly. In fact, I'm going to take some 'me' time, as you call it, this evening. I promise you don't need to worry. Give Daddy a kiss for me and I will call you tomorrow." She doesn't need to know the "me" time I'm referring to involves a good book and an early bedtime. One little white lie to alleviate her worry won't hurt anyone.

I can hear the relief in her voice as she says her goodbye.

Hanging up the phone, I pick up the list Chad left on my desk of places that have lost-and-found boxes ready for me to go through. Lost-and-founds around the city are part of a project I began when I started working here. I set up agreements with different local businesses for them to set aside items from their lost-and-founds that may be useful for our organization. Every week, my co-worker and best friend, Chad, makes a list for which places I will hit up for the week. When I turn this week's list over, I can't hold back the laugh that bursts out of me when I see the last item on it.

Chad is a lot like my mom, always supportive but tirelessly trying to add a little more fun into my life. Just below Faulk Central Library, in all caps he wrote, *LOOKING FOR LOVE IN ALL THE RIGHT PLACES, WITH CHAD AT HANGAR ON 4TH STREET: 7:30 PM.*

Shaking my head, I dial his extension. "You are relentless, you know," I say as he picks up the phone.

"And you love me for it!" he exclaims with his usual enthusiasm.

4

Chad is anything if persistent. And he is right; I do love him for it.

"I'll meet you on one condition," I state plainly.

"I'm willing to meet any condition, buttercup, as long as you meet me and have a good time," he replies before I can even get my condition out.

"I will have a great time as long as you don't force me on every good-looking guy over six feet," I declare.

"Deal, as long as you force me on every good-looking guy over six feet! Now get your cute little ass out the door, so you have time to pretty yourself up! Ciao, Bella!"

I'm still laughing as the phone clicks in my ear.

Standing up, I stretch one last time before I grab my bag and head out the door. I guess my idea for an early bedtime has just flown out the window. I smile to myself as I stuff the lost-and-found list in my bag and make my way to my car.

I've crossed four lost-and-found box stops off my list, and I'm working on the last one for the night when I check my phone. There's a text from Chad lighting up my screen.

Chad: *You better not be late and you better not have that same high school librarian cardigan on that you wore today!*
Me: *What is wrong with my cardigan?*

I look down at my outfit and frown. Well, it was fifteen hours ago when I put it on. I sigh.

Chad: *Don't make me hurt you.*
Me: *Never mind. I see your point. And don't worry. I won't be late. See ya soon! Muah!*

As I stick my phone back into my bag, I notice a large box behind the counter just before Marylou picks it up. This stop won't be as quick as I hoped.

She turns with the box in her arms and smiles. "It's loaded this week, Tessa. I hope you have a little time."

"Thanks, I can make time," I tell Marylou as she hands me the large box over the counter.

Marylou has been the head librarian at Faulk Central for twenty years and was thrilled when I first came to her with the shelter's lost-and-found idea. It is unbelievable all the things people leave behind and never claim.

Walking over to my usual tucked away spot, I dump its contents out and take a seat to begin sorting through it. I divide up the items, grabbing the things that will be of obvious use and placing the things of no use back into the box.

I've been at this nearly an hour when I notice a small black faded notebook. It isn't anything I would typically pay attention to. It's not like it will be beneficial to the shelter and our needs. When I pick it up, I hesitate, feeling a little bit nervous.

I open it up closer to the middle of the journal, skimming the words and taking in the small, precise handwriting. My first thought is that it's a guy's handwriting. As I skim over the words, I feel an unfamiliar sensation burning deep in my chest. The words are calling to some deeper part of me that has yet to make itself known.

The light she shines in my life is my guide...

I flip the pages, catching a glimpse into a life unknown to me.

She makes me want...I want her. I want to be good. I want to be better...

These words make me want, too. They make me want, but I'm not sure what. I realize I should close the notebook. These are private words. Private thoughts not meant for my eyes, but only the eyes of the person who wrote them. Suddenly, I feel a little sad these emotions are here, on this paper, in this box. These are lost words, and I wonder if he feels their absence.

Turning the pages back to the beginning, I look for a name written on the inside cover.

I don't find one—only an address, and I wonder if it's his. If so, would he still be there? Would he want this back? I feel compelled to find out, so I stick the notebook in my bag with intentions of returning it to its owner as soon as I finish sorting through the box.

As I finish up and return the box to Marylou, my mind drifts back to his words. I hear them in my mind, and I can't help wanting to read more. It's like his feelings were written to me even though I know that thought is ridiculous. Before I pick my things back up, I glance at my watch and realize I have very little time to return this book, change clothes, and meet Chad on time. I also realize if I don't return this book, I'll be distracted all night.

Returning this journal seemed like a great idea until now. As I stand outside this door, I almost laugh at how ridiculous this situation is. I mean, what will I even say?

I begin to imagine the conversation once I work up the nerve to knock on this stranger's door. *Hey, so I found your journal…it moved me…and, well, I just had to return it. I imagine you were devastated to have lost it. Who is the girl? Do you truly love her like this? Is love like this possible? I'm so jealous.*

I slap my hand over my mouth as if I just spoke those words out loud. *Jealous? Whoa, get a grip, Tessa. Just return the journal and leave.* I raise my fist, bang it against the door, and notice some of the blue paint comes loose. I watch it float slowly to the porch.

I count to myself, a trick I learned when I was about eight, to help calm my nerves. And right now my nerves are creating havoc in my chest.

No answer. I knock a little harder this time. After I glance down at my watch, I realize I've been here nearly ten minutes, and no one has come to the door. He isn't home, and I can't help the feeling of disappointment.

What do I do? I'm not even sure this is his address. I know I keep thinking I'm looking for a guy, but maybe it isn't. Maybe a girl wrote these words. Either way, I don't know if the owner lives here or not, so I can't just leave it here on a stranger's doorstep.

I'll just leave a note. Decision made, I dig into my bag and pull out some sticky notes and a pen.

Hi

It's probably weird finding a sticky note from a stranger on your door, but I found this journal in the lost-and-found. Your address was inside the cover. I'm not just going to leave it, but if you lost a journal then email me at the email below. If it isn't yours, then...well, then don't email me.

Thanks.

My email: tmc@hoh-ATX.com

TC

I stick it on the door, only hesitating a moment before leaving. I have thirty minutes before I need to meet Chad for my stress-free, fun-filled night. The only problem is I think my mind is going to be on a small notebook and the words of an unknown person.

July 4th, 2005

I think I finally convinced Sara to love me back. It was the moment I ran my fingertip down her cheek that I knew. I saw it reflected in her eyes. The excitement of the moment. Fireworks going off above our heads in celebration of independence. Fireworks. Exploding. Colorful. Bright. That is what my love for her feels like. One beautiful, chaotic, colorful feeling. She is the bright in my life. Her smile lights up my days. We may be young, but isn't young love the best? My mama says my heart is from an old soul. Maybe she's right, but all I know is I feel everything, especially my love for Sara.

CHAPTER 2

Lenox

ARE YOU KIDDING ME?

I read the sticky note I just found on my front door for the third time. Is this a joke? It's been a little over six months since I misplaced that damn journal. Actually, it's been six months since I walked away from it. I grimace at what a fucking lovesick fool I was then.

It's been twenty-six weeks. One hundred eighty-three days. Four thousand three hundred and eighty hours. Two hundred sixty-two thousand eight hundred minutes. Wow. I'm pathetic.

It doesn't matter how you look at it. It has been long enough. Sufficient time has passed to wake up from that mess of a relationship, and now it is rearing its ugly head. Those words are proof of the pansy ass that I used to be. That I never want to be again. Correction: that I *will* never be again. Ever.

Apparently, this "TC" person feels I need these thoughts back. These feelings back. Well, they're wrong.

As I walk into the house, I crumple up the note and toss it in the direction of the trash can. I don't even come close, but I leave it lying on the floor instead of picking it up. I walk to the cabinet and pull out a glass, filling it with water.

Leaning back against the counter, I take a long drink of the cold liquid, hoping it will relieve my dry throat. Thinking about that journal and the things I felt for Sara causes me to feel again. At one time, it was love and longing. Now, I feel sick that I allowed myself to be so weak. As the last drop of water slides into my mouth, the sticky note lying on the floor catches my attention from the corner of my eye, taunting me. Son of a bitch.

Who is this girl? How did she find my journal?

Closing my eyes, I release a sigh. Sara. We met at school when we were sixteen. I was captivated by her smile and the mischievous gleam in her eye. I should have stayed away. It took me ten years to realize what I knew all along; she wouldn't be mine for forever. And she wasn't. I'm not sure she ever was.

When she left, my only link to her was that journal. Then I walked away from it. I just stood up and left it sitting on a table in that library without a backward glance. I nearly destroyed everything around me trying to get over that girl. To get over that life. I retraced our whole relationship, but it was gone and with it the memory of the girl who stomped on my heart. Well, those memories can stay buried for all I care.

Glancing at the clock on the wall, I realize I better get moving if I'm going to meet up with Sammy on time.

I'm sitting alone at one of the outdoor picnic tables with my head down, and my hand threaded through my hair, staring into my beer.

I've barely touched it. Sammy went to get another one for himself, making snide comments as he walked away about how I'm being a dick tonight. Maybe I am.

I just can't seem to shake this feeling. I've always liked control. I lost it with Sara. I swore I would never lose it again. Except tonight, for the first time in nearly six months, I feel it slipping.

Something as simple as a note on a pink sticky note has sent my mind into a tailspin. Fuck this. I pick up my beer and slam it back. *Ah, that feels better.* The rush the beer sends through me provides me momentary relief.

Before I know it, Sammy is at my side placing another pint of ale in front of me. I told him I didn't need another one, but he got one regardless. Thank God. I pick this one up without looking at him and slam it back, too. I see Sammy shake his head at me from the corner of my eye.

"Dude, what the hell is wrong with you?" he asks as he takes a seat across from me. "I'm not getting you another one until I drink mine."

I look right at him. "I can get my own damn beer."

Without responding, he takes a slow drink. The crowd around us gets thicker as the time gets closer to the band's first set. Sammy's eyes never leave mine.

"What the fuck is up, Nox? You're a dick tonight." He pauses and takes another drink. "I haven't seen you act like such a douche-bag since Sa—"

"Don't you fucking say her name," I tell him, frustration hugging every word.

He holds his hands up. "Damn, man. I thought you were over that shit."

I blow out a long, frustrated sigh. He's right. I'm a dick. All because of some words I wrote in a journal and the feelings that I lost with them.

"I am. It's just tonight that chapter has reopened, and I'm not sure how to handle it."

"What does that mean, man?" he asks, concern in his voice. Sammy helped pick me up when Sara left, wrecking my world.

Yeah, what does that mean? The sounds of conversations fill the air, laughter between friends, the shuffling of feet all around me, and I can't even enjoy my beer. I can say for sure I'm over Sara. I just can't explain why knowing that someone out there has my journal—my thoughts—has me feeling so out of control.

"I don't know, Sammy. I just don't know." I stand up to get another drink. "The band is about to go on. Do you want another one?" I ask him as I point to his drink.

He looks down at his beer then back at me. "Sure, man. Thanks."

I can see it in his eyes. Sammy wants to ask me more, but he won't. He knows me well enough to let this go. The only question is, will I be able to do the same?

The crowd is dispersing as the bartender makes the last call for alcohol over the microphone.

Tonight, I put everything I had into forgetting the feelings floating through my mind since I got home from work. All I have to show for it, though, are slurred speech and slightly blurry vision.

Sammy slaps me on my back, taking me off guard as we walk through the doors of the bar and back into the night air. I stumble forward, barely catching myself from falling flat on my face.

"Dude, even though you were acting like an asshole most of the night, that band was fucking amazing." His words are slightly garbled.

I don't respond, ignoring his dig at me, so he keeps on talking. We make our way down the sidewalk, Sammy rambling on and on, something about tonight's music, but I can't focus on his words. I can only concentrate on each staggering step I take, trying to avoid every person we pass.

A fucking pink sticky note. What the fuck? Who writes a note on a little sticky like they are carrying a complete conversation with a person and leave it at their front door? Fucking pink sticky note.

I suddenly stop. "Dude, did you call Uber?"

Sammy, still rambling, stops a few feet ahead of me, only now realizing I'm straggling behind. Looking back, he asks, "What?"

Trying to focus, I say again, "Did you call Uber?"

"No, didn't you?" he replies.

I stare at him. Sammy seems to be swaying like a tree in the wind.

"Nope," I finally respond.

We both continue to stare at one another. People are passing between us, too involved to walk around us, carrying on conversations as if we aren't even here. Maybe if I stare at him long enough, he will call. I think my phone is in my pocket, but I'm not sure, and my hand feels too heavy to lift. Finally, I win, and Sammy pulls his phone out.

"Asshole," I hear him whisper under his breath. I smirk.

I walk toward him, people still passing by me, people being careful to avoid touching me as we pass. It's hard to keep my coordination when my head is spinning—spinning from the alcohol I consumed, spinning because of memories awakened that were better left buried in the past. All because of TC. Whoever the hell that is.

At that very moment, my shoulder collides with another, whirling me around. Lifting my eyes, I catch another pair looking at me. Blinking. I can't make out their features through my hazy gaze, but the eyes are female. It's only a brief moment, but she's staring too. Blink. Neither of us says a word, and she keeps moving farther away. Blink. Blink. I feel a tug in my middle as if a string connects us, the brief brush of our shoulders linking us together. Suddenly, the tether snaps when Sammy grabs hold of my shoulder. My eyes dart away and back again. Her friend is turning her around and pulling on her arm.

"Uber. Greatest fucking invention ever." Pushing me toward the curb, Sammy laughs. "Get in, jackass."

Taking one more glance down the sidewalk before I get in the car, I see her glance back, only able to make out her silhouette because the alcohol is still coursing through me. Damn it.

"Get in, asshole!" Sammy is still trying to push me in.

As I glare back at him, two things cross my mind: First, I'm going to beat Sammy's ass. Second, that fucking pink sticky note.

February 6th, 2006

I wrote her a love note and gave her a single rose. It isn't quite Valentine's day, but I don't particularly like the idea of celebrating being in love on one day for the whole year. My asshole friends gave me a hard time and said I'm whipped. Maybe I am. I don't care. I'm sixteen, nearly seventeen, and I'm in love. I watched her read the words I wrote, a blush coloring her cheeks, a smile touching her lips. Her beautiful, soft lips. I love her lips. I love the way her face reveals what she is feeling. We still haven't said the words, but I know she feels them, too. I can see what Sara and I have be-yond today. Each day with her makes my future look brighter.

CHAPTER 3

TESSA

MAYBE IF I JUST LIE here and don't move, it won't hurt so much.

Damn Chad and his compelling ways. His idea of loosening up is all fun and games until the next morning. When will I learn to say no? Or at least, stop. My head throbs when I dare to open one eye and see the sunlight glaring through the window.

Moaning, I roll over, burying my head in the pillow.

One tequila. Two tequila. Three tequila. I lost count after that. Luckily, I didn't hit the floor, as the saying goes. I remember stumbling my way down Sixth Street back to Chad's place so I could call for a ride. I'm not sure how we made it, winding our way through the usual Saturday night crowd as I clung to his side, but we did without any disasters. I suddenly remember the game we played, trying to avoid touching strangers.

One simple rule: no touching. I was confident I would win. A little harrowing laugh escapes me but is suddenly cut short at the memory of Chad pulling me toward him, laughing. The memory is foggy. I looked at him for a moment, and he was smiling. I lost.

A funny sensation runs through me and up my arm.

The encounter was so brief and mundane, yet there was more to it. Even through my drunken haze, I felt more than a mere brush of a stranger's shoulder. When I looked back, my eyes were unable to focus. I try to remember his face. I can't. The shock left me stunned, but as quickly as it happened, it was over. One of those fleeting moments of chance stolen from us.

An unexpected sadness spreads through my chest, a dull ache. *Damn it, what is wrong with me?* It was nothing. I'm acting silly.

Let it go, Tessa.

My phone rings, bringing me back to the present. Back to the world of rational thinking.

Reaching blindly out to the nightstand, while my head remains beneath the pillow, I grip my phone and pull it into the darkness with me. Glancing at the screen, I smile as I hit the talk button.

"Why did you do this to me?" I say without even a hello.

"I have no clue what you mean. It could be because a good portion of my brain cells are dead," Chad says into the phone.

I can hear the regret of our adventure in the tone of his voice. He is in pain, too. I want to laugh, but I hold it in. Any movement is agony.

"Tess, just making sure you're alive. I'm hanging up now. Ciao." *Click.*

Did he just hang up on me? Really? His concern for my well-being is so touching. I look at the phone as if I can see Chad through it. Rolling my eyes, I place the phone back on the nightstand. Ugh. I need water. Badly.

I realize I must look ridiculous sliding from under the covers off the side of the bed, but I'm not sure I can stand up just yet. Sitting on the floor, while the side of the bed holds up my fifty-pound head, I contemplate how long I can sit here without the food and water I so desperately need. Before I can make any life-or-death decisions, I hear the musical sound of an incoming text message on my phone.

Ugh. If it's Chad again, I'm going to bitch slap his ass.

My brain is trying to tell my arm to move, but it isn't quite able to trigger any movement. Since when do all of my body parts weigh so much? I want to cry. Maybe if I cry, then I can drink my tears, and I won't need to move. Wait. What? Dear Lord, am I still drunk?

I close my eyes, but before I can get too relaxed, my phone sings again. Ugh.

A couple of minutes pass and I reach out, knocking my phone and the small "lost and found" journal to the floor. The one that consumed my thoughts last night until José drowned them. I blink a few times to focus my throbbing head. Picking up the journal first, I open it, flipping the pages to the center.

Sara's voice whispers to me even when she is not here. Her smile brightens my day, although the sky is full of clouds. I'm obsessed, and I want you to possess me. Oh, Sara. She has stolen me.

I skim the last statement over and over. *She has stolen me.* The words hold a sort of sadness. I can't put my finger on it, but all of his words carry hidden meaning and emotion. I don't recognize them because I've never felt obsessed, nor has anyone ever possessed me. A little of the sadness creeps into my own mind, and I release a long, heavy sigh. Pathetic. I almost wish Chad were sitting with me again with a little bit of José. Assholes. Once again, my phone plays a tune.

Lifting my phone, I swipe my finger across the screen and see an email notification pop up.

It isn't a text as I thought. It's an email. It's too early to be checking work emails. But it isn't work. In fact, it's from an email address I don't recognize.

To: tmc@hoh-ATX.com
From: lmmusic@rewind.com
Subject: Journal

TC,
First, who leaves notes on a stranger's
door...and on a pink sticky note? Second,
the journal is mine. Was mine. I don't
want it. Throw it away. Thanks.

    The words seem to sober me up pretty quickly. What the hell?
This couldn't be written by the same guy. Rude. And...and inconsid-
erate. And, rude. I read it again. Jackass. The sharp pang in my head
intensifies as I read it once more. I begin furiously typing a reply.

To: lmmusic@rewind.com
From: tmc@hoh-ATX.com
Subject: RE: Journal

Good morning to you. You're rude and a
liar. You can't be the same person who
wrote those words. I think I'll just hold
on to it.

To: tmc@hoh-ATX.com
From: lmmusic@rewind.com
Subject: RE: RE: Journal

Are you kidding me? First the pink sticky
note and now name calling? It's mine.
Throw. It. Away.

To: lmmusic@rewind.com
From: tmc@hoh-ATX.com
Subject: RE: RE: RE: Journal

First, why does it matter what color
sticky note I use? I happen to be partial
to pink. Second, if you haven't already
guessed by my initial salutation, I think
you're lying. And, an asshole. Yep, a
big, lying asshole.

Ha. There. I told him. I'm feeling more confident that I won his
game. Then my phone chimes again. Ugh.

To: tmc@hoh-ATX.com
From: lmmusic@rewind.com
Subject: RE: RE: RE: RE: Journal…

Salutation? Who are you? Do you know what
year this is? And the insult. Asshole? If
it weren't true, I'd be crushed. Sorry to
disappoint you, but again, the journal is
mine. Trash it. Signed, The Lying Asshole

Excuse me? Is he making fun of me? He's making fun of me. I
frown. What is his problem? He insists the journal is his. Feeling in-
dignant, I open the small black book and skim the words again.
Nope. Still don't believe him. I'm ending this little exchange right
now. Asshole. My frown deepens. I wish I could think of something
more insulting than *asshole*. Ugh.

To: lmmusic@rewind.com
From: tmc@hoh-ATX.com
Subject: RE: RE: RE: RE: RE: Journal…

Excuse me, Mr. Lying Asshole. I still don't believe you. I'm keeping the journal until I find its rightful owner. Buh bye.

I hit send and do my best maniacal laugh. Not a good idea. Grabbing my head, I try to hold the pulsating pain still to keep my head attached to my neck. Although, it may be better if I just let my head fall off, and I grow a new one. My ex-best friend Chad and his accomplice José are officially on my hate list.

Only second on the list to the lying asshole.

August 13, 2006

It's the end of summer. We spent nearly every day together. Every waking minute. School will be starting in a little over a week. I can't wait for her delicate hand to be in mine as we walk down the hall. I'll feel her heart beating with her palm to mine, connecting us as the rhythm of it sings to me. I feel proud and lucky to have her. My mom says slow down, but I don't know how to slow down my heart when it comes to Sara.

CHAPTER
4

Lenox

I CAN'T HELP THE LAUGH that escapes when I read the email that just came through on my phone.

Who is this girl? I was still so fucking worked up over the idea someone found my journal that I figured if I emailed, then I could end this whole frustrating situation. Instead, I find myself wanting more. I can't explain it, but I'm enjoying annoying the shit out of this girl. And annoying her is exactly what I'm doing. I imagine every word in this email was typed out with hard pounding motions. Ha. She's pissed.

What's even more fascinating to me is the fact she doesn't believe the journal is mine.

Oh, shit. She doesn't think the journal is mine; I repeat to myself. I read her words again, really letting them sink in. She's keeping the journal. She's fucking keeping the journal, and she is going to continue searching for the owner. Searching for me. Damn it.

My head falls back on the couch; suddenly a purring sound vibrates in my ear.

Reaching my hands behind my head, I pull the fluffy ball of fur around and hold it against me.

"Roosevelt, I think I'm in major fucking trouble," I whisper to the cat as I run my hand over his soft coat.

Someone clears their throat from behind me. Startled, I jump off the couch. My mother is standing near the front door, hands on her hips, tapping her foot.

"Lenox Malone, you better watch that filthy mouth of yours. I taught you better than that."

"Shit, Mom. Don't sneak up on me like that," I say and cringe when I see her eyebrows shoot up when another curse word leaves my mouth.

"Look here, my little man child. I didn't sneak up. I knocked... more than once. I knew you were home, although you didn't answer. So I let myself in with my key." She walks over to me and brushes the hair from my eyes like I'm still her eight-year-old little boy. "I thought you might be asleep."

My eyes soften as I take in the woman who raised me. Kristin Malone was one tough and incredibly brave woman. She was young when she had me. Young and alone. It was just the two of us my whole life, and while I longed for a male figure in my life, I never felt like I didn't have everything I needed. Reaching out, I pull her into a tight hug. I hadn't seen her in a few weeks; our schedules have been so out of sync. She began working night shifts at the hospital, so she spends most of her days sleeping.

Pushing back from her, we smile at one another.

"So what brings you by today?" I ask, taking my seat back on the couch next to Roosevelt, who doesn't even lift his head in acknowledgment.

"Well, I thought you might want to have lunch today. It's been a few weeks, and I don't have to be back on until tomorrow night." She begins picking up a few glasses I've left lying around the house.

"Seriously, Mom. Stop. You don't have to come over and do my dishes." I stand up again and take the glasses from her, taking them to the sink. "As for lunch, I would love to. My stomach can probably handle a little food now."

"Out late last night, were we?" She laughs as she rubs Roosevelt's head. Damn cat is spoiled.

"A bit." Laughing, I grab my shoes and begin putting them on my feet. "Of course, Sammy and I had a contest over who could consume the most Sierra Nevada in one night. I can't tell you who won. If the way I feel today is any indication, I would say neither of us did." We both laugh and my mind drifts to the night before.

I was looking to drown my irritation over the damn resurrection of my past. I did just that, and if I remember correctly, Sammy and I could barely put one foot in front of the other. I'm not sure how we called Uber and made it is as far as we did without falling on our asses or knocking some else down along…wait.

My mind explodes with blurry images of a girl. The scent of lilac. An almost debilitating electric current that passed between us as our shoulders brushed against one another. Good God, what was that? I can't remember her face. I don't even think I ever actually saw her clearly. I just remember feeling her. Her scent. I felt her all the way to the center of my stomach. It almost hurts thinking about it. What the fuck?

"Lenox…Earth to Lenox," my mom says as she waves her hand in front of my face.

Turning my gaze up to hers, I notice a concerned expression move across her features. Shit, I've seen that look before. She is about to Mommy-pounce on me.

"Sorry, Mom…just thinking about something that happened last night." I give her a smile to reassure her that I'm okay.

"Are you sure you're up to having lunch? We can do dinner instead, or wait for another day altogether." Her voice is sounding less concerned than before, but still motherly.

"Nope. I'm all right. So where do you want to go?" I ask as I stand and grab my wallet off the kitchen table.

Tapping her finger on her chin, she looks at me with a huge

smile on her face. "Hut's Hamburgers. I've been craving a chocolate milkshake and the Beach Boys' favorite."

I laugh out loud. Sometimes, I wonder who the kid is and who the parent is. She walks over to me and loops her arm through mine.

"I love you, Mom."

"Love you, too. Now feed your mother and fill me in on what's been going on in your life."

I smile, but I feel a little squeeze in the pit of my stomach. I think, *Oh, you know, annoying girls with pink sticky notes. Ghost from the past. And a missed encounter with a stranger.* All of which are making me feel things I don't want to feel anymore.

May 29, 2007

It's been a little over two years since I lost my heart to Sara. Two years since life got a little sweeter. I turned eighteen a month ago. I'm eighteen and still so in love. In love with long, flowing hair. In love with soft, creamy skin. In love with an innocent, kind heart. In love with... Sara. She gave me the best gift I could have asked for today. She said she loved me. I was finally able to tell her what has been in my heart since the moment I met her. She cried. I love you, Sara.

CHAPTER 5

TESSA

WEDNESDAY. HUMP DAY. I'VE ALWAYS hated that term. I mean, really? Hump day? I groan. I've had a headache all day, and the fact that my week is already halfway over doesn't make me feel better. In fact, I'm more stressed about everything I need to accomplish by Friday.

Shuffling the stacks of paper around on my desk, I try to figure out where I laid last month's statistics. "Damn it. Where did I put it?" I say to myself...or, so I thought.

The sound of a voice coming through the doorway to my office startles me.

"You do realize that no matter how many times you move those piles around on your desk, what you're looking for isn't going to appear magically," Chad stated sarcastically. A small smile plays at the corners of his mouth as he props himself up against the door jam.

Looking back down at the chaos displayed before me, I slowly lower my forehead onto the edge of my desk. I release a long drawn out sigh.

I hear Chad walk farther into my office until his feet pop into view next to me. I don't even bother looking up. He bends down, looking under my arms. I tilt my head slightly in his direction until our eyes meet.

"Sweetie, whatcha doin'?" He blinks a couple of times before continuing. "You're acting a bit distracted and crazy this week. It's beginning to make me nervous."

"It's not that bad," I mumble.

He lightly pats me on my head. "Oh, okay," he says sardonically. "You said, 'Huh?' five times in the meeting this morning. Senile Sue was more aware of the conversation than you were, and we know that isn't good."

Sue is our eighty-five-year-old receptionist, who volunteers nearly every day. She is sweet if not a bit forgetful and hard of hearing.

A laugh escapes me as I roll my eyes. "We both know you're exaggerating a bit on that point."

Standing back up, he grunts. "I don't exaggerate." He walks away, and I know he's leaving me to my pity party. "Say what you want, but you're distracted and tired. I say a long weekend is the only cure. You've been working too hard."

I hear the door close then suddenly reopen. "Oh, and Tess? You can't be here to save them all."

The door creaks shut once more, and I'm alone again, contemplating Chad's accuracy about what I'm feeling and how I can't deny it.

Several hours later, I'm relaxed on my cushy chenille sofa. A cup of hot chamomile tea is steaming in one hand, and my favorite Mia Sheridan novel is in the other.

Ah, this is just what I needed. A good book. No worries. No interrupt—

Well, so much for that, I think as a jingle sounds from my phone sitting on the coffee table. Ignore it, Tessa. It isn't important. Emails can wait until tomorrow.

I turn the page and sigh. Archer is so dreamy. I've always wondered if you could fall in love with someone having never heard their voice. Sigh.

Another jingle. And another. Ugh. Fine. I really should turn off my notifications once I get home. Setting my cup and book on the table next to me, I reach over and pick up my phone. Swiping the screen, I tap my inbox icon. Are you freaking kidding me?

```
To: tmc@hoh-ATX.com
From: lmmusic@rewind.com
Subject: Hi, it's me again

Salutations.
Did you throw it away?
```

Ugh. Is he trying to be funny? I want to be annoyed yet feel my mouth threaten to break into a smile. I read the next message.

```
To: tmc@hoh-ATX.com
From: lmmusic@rewind.com
Subject: RE: Hi, it's me again

Seriously, TC, I hope you tossed the damn
journal and moved on.
```

Oh my God. This guy just won't quit. He's persistent. Maybe this journal is his…I mean, why would he lie about it. I don't like the idea. The guy who wrote those words in the notebook has to be kind and romantic. This guy isn't. Nope. I'm not listening to him. I refuse to believe it's him. I tap out my simple reply.

```
To: lmmusic@rewind.com
From: tmc@hoh-ATX.com
Subject: RE: RE: Hi, It's me again

Ugh. You're so rude. And, no. No, I ha-
ven't thrown it away.
```

I grin. The response is almost immediate.

```
To: tmc@hoh-ATX.com
From: lmmusic@rewind.com
Subject: RE: RE: RE: RE: Hi, It's me
again

Dear God, you're stubborn. I'm going to
regret this, but may I ask why?
```

What? Is he insulting me? And I don't have to tell him my reasons. I quickly respond.

To: lmmusic@rewind.com
From: tmc@hoh-ATX.com
Subject: Go away!

Only the owner of the journal in question
can tell me what to do with it.

To: tmc@hoh-ATX.com
From: lmmusic@rewind.com
Subject: Ridiculous

I am the owner.

To: lmmusic@rewind.com
From: tmc@hoh-ATX.com
Subject: Lies

I don't believe you.

To: tmc@hoh-ATX.com
From: lmmusic@rewind.com
Subject: Believe it

This is getting ridiculous. You are ridiculous.

    Now he thinks I'm ridiculous. Am I acting ridiculous? *You're absolutely ridiculous,* whispers the tiny voice in my head. I'm not sure why this whole thing even matters. I should just throw it away.

It would be easier than dealing with this guy. A thought pops into my head. Maybe it belongs to the person who lived at that address before him.

To: lmmusic@rewind.com
From: tmc@hoh-ATX.com
Subject: Question

Did you move into your house recently? I mean, it's possible the journal belongs to the person who lived there before you.

Within seconds, a response pops up.

To: tmc@hoh-ATX.com
From: lmmusic@rewind.com
Subject: Stubborn

Are you serious? No. I didn't just move in. I moved in three years ago when I graduated college. This house was my grandparents'. I don't understand what you need from me to convince you. Where did you say you found it again?

I stare at the message. Could he be lying?

To: lmmusic@rewind.com
From: tmc@hoh-ATX.com
Subject: Who are you calling stubborn?

Yes. I'm serious. And I found it in the lost and found at Faulk Central Library.

To: tmc@hoh-ATX.com
From: lmmusic@rewind.com
Subject: You're scary

Do you make it a habit of digging through lost and founds?

To: lmmusic@rewind.com
From: tmc@hoh-ATX.com
Subject: Not that I should explain

Actually, I do. It's part of my job to go through old lost and found items around town.

Silence. Maybe he has given up this charade. I stare at my phone, waiting. The weird thing is I want to know what he is going to say in response to my last email. Still nothing. He's going to leave me hanging. This is so annoying. The jingle alerting me to a new text startles me, and I drop my phone. Shit. Leaning forward, I reach down and pick my phone up from the floor. I read the screen.

To: tmc@hoh-ATX.com
From: lmmusic@rewind.com
Subject: Curious

What do you mean it's your job? Your job
is to dig through strangers' lost posses-
sions?

I guess we're going to keep the conversation going after all.

To: lmmusic@rewind.com
From: tmc@hoh-ATX.com
Subject: Are we still talking?

That's what I said; it's my job.

I can't fight the urge to argue with him, and I don't like confron-
tation. He just does something to me. This stranger intrigues me and
exasperates me at the same time. I'm never intrigued or exasperated.

To: tmc@hoh-ATX.com
From: lmmusic@rewind.com
Subject: You've done it

I can't help myself. You've piqued my interest. What kind of job sends someone
around town searching through lost and
found boxes?

Really? As if I'm going to tell him where I work. I'm not stupid. How do I respond? I could just ignore him. Or not. Well, if we get technical, he didn't actually ask where I work, but instead, he asked what I do. That's different. I'll just answer this one question and ask him to leave me alone.

To: lmmusic@rewind.com
From: tmc@hoh-ATX.com
Subject: RE: You've piqued my interest

It's only one aspect of my job, but I look for items that have gone unclaimed for more than a month that will benefit people who are less fortunate.

To: tmc@hoh-ATX.com
From: lmmusic@rewind.com
Subject: RE: RE: You've piqued my interest

Impressive.

To: lmmusic@rewind.com
From: tmc@hoh-ATX.com
Subject: RE: RE: RE: You've piqued my interest

There's no need for sarcasm.

To: tmc@hoh-ATX.com
From: lmmusic@rewind.com
Subject: RE: RE: RE: RE: You've piqued my interest

I'm not sarcastic. It's impressive. But I'm not sure how my journal helps the less fortunate improve their lives.

To: lmmusic@rewind.com
From: tmc@hoh-ATX.com
Subject: RE: RE: RE: RE: RE: You've piqued my interest

It doesn't. I just…

To: tmc@hoh-ATX.com
From: lmmusic@rewind.com
Subject: RE: RE: RE: RE: RE: RE: You've piqued my interest

You just?

To: lmmusic@rewind.com
From: tmc@hoh-ATX.com
Subject: RE: RE: RE: RE: RE: RE: RE: You've piqued my interest

I don't have to explain. I still don't believe it's yours.

To: tmc@hoh-ATX.com
From: lmmusic@rewind.com
Subject: Still being stubborn

Really? Are you always this stubborn?

To: lmmusic@rewind.com
From: tmc@hoh-ATX.com
Subject: RE: Stubborn

Are you?

Seriously, Tessa. You sound like a bitch. Just let this go. I'm not sure why I'm acting this way. I guess I don't want it to be his because he dismisses it so quickly and I can't. It makes me feel things. Things I've never felt. Glancing back down at my phone, I read the email that just popped up.

To: tmc@hoh-ATX.com
From: lmmusic@rewind.com
Subject: amended...crazy not stubborn

You're crazy, lady. Throw my journal away.

Crazy? This whole situation is a little crazy. I toss my phone to the other end of the sofa and ignore it for the rest of the night. I'm tired. Tired of thinking. Tired of feeling. Tired of searching for something I can't quite understand.

July 15, 2007

Two months have almost passed. Two months that Sara has known that I love her. Two months since the gate guarding my heart opened and my love for her came flooding out. This feeling. I never want it to end. My mom still says to be careful, that I'm young, and life can change in the blink of an eye. She says young love is the hardest to hold on to, and she doesn't want to see me hurt. I love my mom. She's speaking from experience because my dad left her. Left us. Sara and I aren't my parents. Sara loves me, and I love her. I have to trust what I'm feeling. I don't know any other way.

CHAPTER 6

Lenox

SHE'S CRAZY. AND FRUSTRATING. TWO of my least favorite qualities in a person. So why am I so intrigued by her? Why do I feel like I want to know more about her?

Thoughts of this girl kept me up all night. The way she refuses to believe me. Especially when there isn't any logical reason for me to lie. Her snarky remarks. What is it? Blinking my eyes so they can adjust to the morning sunlight streaming through the blinds, it hits me. The journal.

I can't understand why she is so protective of it. It doesn't make sense that she is so passionate about finding the owner. Damn it. I'm the owner. Those are my words. My feelings. I doubt myself—doubt something I know to be true. All because of her. I think maybe that's it. Her doubts and the fact she feels so much for this stupid journal have me curious about the person who is behind these absurd and exasperating emails.

Throwing the covers back, I roll out of bed and stretch my arms over my head. This is going to be a long day.

Just as I thought, the day is dragging. On three different occasions, a customer stood staring at me, waiting for a reply to a question I hadn't even heard them ask. I need this to be over. Not just the work day, but this whole obsession with an annoying girl who refuses to throw away my memories better left buried.

"Dude! What the hell is your issue today?" Sammy says as he slaps me on the back, startling me from another daydream.

Sighing, I run my hand over the back of my head and down my face, trying to clear my mind. Looking up at Sammy, I blow out a breath. "I didn't get much sleep."

"Seriously, Nox...man, is everything okay?" he asks, a concerned look on his face. "You've been off for nearly a week."

I want to tell Sammy so he can put this in perspective, but he'll probably make more out of it than should be. Not to mention, he'll make it all about Sara and the funny thing is she is the furthest thing from my mind. Wow, that feels good. I remember a time this would've been all about Sara.

"Dude, you're weird," I hear Sammy say.

Glancing up, I notice he's giving me a strange look.

"Uh, what?" I ask.

"You've been a freak all day, daydreaming, looking as if you're anywhere but here, and now you're smiling like the fucking Cheshire cat. What gives?" He continues filing away albums in their rightful place in the bins along the wall.

"Remember the other night when we were out?" I ask, stretching my arms overhead. My whole body feels in knots.

"You mean when you were acting like a dick?"

I let out a huff. Leave it to Sammy to call me out.

"Yeah. I had my reasons, and it wasn't anything personal. You asked if it was about Sara, and well, it was...is...sort of. Some girl found my journal. A journal filled with words about Sara and our relationship. One I thought I lost and was happy to have gone." I explain.

"So what, you're missing Sara again? It's opened up old wounds, and you can't sleep?" He turns with his hands resting on his hips, looking at me. "I thought you were done with that shit, man."

"I am!" I reply all too quickly.

Shaking his head, he says, "yeah, sounds like it."

"Look; you don't get it. It isn't Sara. It's someone else," I confess. Sammy watches me with a confused look on his face. "My journal...the girl who found it. She left her email for me to claim the journal. I did and asked her to throw it away."

"Okay, I don't see the problem," Sammy states.

I sneer at his comment.

"Yeah, well, the issue is she's annoying as hell," I explain.

He continues to stare at me, waiting for more. How in the hell does he always do that? I can never leave anything unsaid without him figuring it out.

"Fine...you're such an asshole. The biggest problem is the fact she refuses to throw it away," I finally admit.

He smiles. "What the fuck? Why not?"

"Because she doesn't believe that I'm the real owner. So we've been exchanging emails." I release a loud sigh. "Let me just say this girl hits all my buttons and it's driving me insane. She is argumentative and infuriating and...and...I can't stop myself from fucking thinking about her."

A blank look on his face, Sammy stares at me for a moment before the corner of his mouth tips up in amusement. He is going to make a fucking big deal about this whole situation. Asshole. I wait for it.

"So you can't stop thinking about her." His smile grows wider. "She's totally hot, isn't she? This girl is crazy, but you don't care that she's crazy because she's hot." Still, his smile grows which seems impossible. I watch him in disgust when suddenly he's pulling me into a hug. "I'm so fucking proud of you."

I'm going to kick his ass.

Pushing his dumbass off of me, I begin to protest. "You're such a douchebag! I haven't even met her. I don't know what she looks like or what her voice sounds like; I only know she has my journal, and she refuses to believe it's mine."

When I glance at him, he appears, even more, amused. I hate being his friend sometimes.

"This girl could totally be a dude," he mocks and begins laughing.

Shaking my head, I turn and walk away. "You're a dick," I declare over my shoulder.

I hear him call from behind me. "Nox....Lenox...wait up! I'm just yanking your chain. Stop, man."

I swipe my badge to clock out and hear him do the same. As we walk out the back door, Sammy clears his throat. "Lenox, seriously, dude. What's really the problem here? It can't only be that this girl has your journal, and she won't throw it away. Who cares that she has your journal?"

I turn back toward him and shrug my shoulders. "I don't know Sam. This girl has gotten under my skin. I feel more arguing with her through emails than I have in the last six months. I don't feel in control of what I'm feeling." I release a long drawn out sigh. "I mean, I haven't even met the girl, but there is an attraction there, I can't explain it. I think maybe if I can just convince her to get rid of that damn journal then I can just go on with my life."

He's watching me; I can see him processing what I just divulged.

Finally, he looks directly into my eyes and slaps my shoulder. "So how do we convince this chick to either throw away your fucking pansy-ass diary or give it back to you so you can do it?"

This guy. I laugh out loud and brush his hand off my shoulder. "I don't know, but you're still a dick."

January 6, 2008

Our first semester of college is over. Our winter break will be over soon, too. The transition was hard, but we made it work. I can see Sara is scared. I'm not. I promised her that nothing would change. I will love her just as much today as I did nearly three years ago. There was something in her eyes that tells me she doesn't believe me. I told her I would convince her. And I will. I will love her every day like it's my last. We've made it this far, and we can make it farther.

CHAPTER 7

TESSA

OVER THE LAST FEW WEEKS, the days have been dragging. I didn't think it was possible for my regular mundane life to get any less exciting, but I was wrong. So wrong.

I've spent nearly every day working up proposals for more funding. It's cut into the time I spend interviewing the new men and women needing help getting off the streets. It's frustrating because I love the hands on part of this job, but the funding is necessary to make it all work.

I drop my purse and kick off my flats as soon as I walk in the door. I don't even care that no one can walk in my apartment without tripping over the wake of my laziness. I'm tired. Drained. Jesus! Not to mention a complete hot mess, I realize as I walk past the mirror hanging on the wall at the end of the hallway. I stop and look into the eyes of a hoary looking twenty-five-year-old. No wonder my mom and Chad are always hounding me about my life and taking care of myself. I'm amazing at taking care of others, but shitty at taking care of myself.

Blinking a few times, I reach up and place my fingertips against the shadows below my eyes.

I can hear Chad's sarcastic comment in my head. *"Dark circles are only cute on raccoons, honey."*

Releasing a sigh, I shuffle my way over to my bed. Too tired to even pull back the floral duvet, I crawl across the bed and allow myself to fall forward. Closing my eyes, I drift off into a much-needed slumber.

He's sitting up next to me on the bed with his back against the headboard as I lie facing him. A soft smile on my face, I listen to him read his latest love note. His long, strong fingers flipping the page as he continues to make love to me with his words.

"Your body curves perfectly into mine; I listen to you sleep. I imagine holding you this way forever. I wonder if I will be so lucky as to have you forever," he whispers to me. I reach out and run my hand delicately down his arm with every intention...

"Sweetheart, you know I love you, but this is never happening." Chad's voice breaks through the clouds of bliss in my mind.

Instantly, I sit straight up in bed with a gasp. My eyes flutter open, taking in my surroundings until they land on Chad stretched out on my bed next to me with his legs crossed at the ankles.

"What the hell, Chad?" I say in mock anger once I get my bearings.

"Oh, honey...your face was classic," he muses.

"What are you doing here? You scared the shit out of me," I scold him.

The humor on his face spreads. "You were thinking about the words in this little black book, weren't you? Buttercup, I felt the poke of Cupid's arrow reading these words, myself. Are you keeping something...someone from me?" Chad inquires in his usual direct manner.

It's only now I notice the journal in his hands. I snatch it from his hands and hold it close to my chest. The look of surprise breaks across his features, which doesn't happen often.

Sitting up a little straighter, he crosses his arms over his chest. "Okay, spill it, lady," he gently demands.

"There's nothing to spill," I state calmly, although the zip of nerves running up my spine tells a different story.

Shaking his head slowly side to side, Chad waits.

"Fine. I found the journal about a month ago in one of the lost and found boxes." I put my hand up to stop him from speaking. "And before you say a word, I'm well aware that this worn-out little book doesn't have a single benefit for our project." Looking down at my hands in my lap, picking the already chipped polish from my nails, I shrug my shoulders. "I can't explain it. There was something about it, so I read a few entries in it. After that, I just couldn't leave it in there... lost."

"So what you're saying is, you have no idea who wrote these words or who it belongs to," He marvels as he points to the small book I'm currently holding to my chest.

"Yes...well, sort of," I answer, biting my lip.

"Oh, no, that answer isn't going to work. I know you, and something is going on so you may as well spill it," he prods.

"I hope you know I hate you," I say without conviction.

"Sure...sure...now speak," he urges.

"Okay. There is an address inside the cover, but no name. I went there to return it, but no one was home. I didn't feel comfortable leaving it, plus if I'm honest I wanted to look into the eyes of the person who wrote the words I read." I pause, waiting for a snide remark from Chad, but he keeps his mouth closed. So I continue, "I left a note with my email, but without my name."

"And?" he asks, waiting for more. He always knows when I'm leaving something out.

"And some guy emailed me, but it can't be him," I confess.

His eyes roam over my face before he asks, "Why can't it be

him?"

"It...it...cannot be him because this guy is rude and unhappy!" I complain.

"How do you know this from one email?" he asks.

I'm feeling so worked up that I don't even notice the smirk resting on Chad's face.

"It wasn't one email! He has been trying to convince me to throw away the journal. Of course, I keep refusing because why would someone who wrote such sweet and romantic things want to throw them away. It isn't him; that's why!" I protest.

Chad is watching me with a full blown grin now. I roll my eyes because I know he is reading way more into this whole situation. How can he do that? I don't even know what the situation is or why I'm a little nutty over the fact this mystery guy and I haven't exchanged a single email in three weeks.

"We need to find this mystery man," he announces.

I look up in shock. "We do? Why?"

"We do and we will," he promises.

A strange, unsettling feeling fills my chest at the prospect of why this sounds even remotely like a good idea. Lying back on the bed, I release a loud sigh. "Have I told you lately how much I hate you?"

He chuckles. "Not as often as you've said that you love me, so I win." Chad lies down next to me and pulls me into a hug.

March 12, 2008

It's spring break, and I'm working. It's how I pay for college,
and it's worth it. My mom hates
I have to work to help her, but
I don't mind. She's done everything for me. Sacrificed everything for me. She feels guilty I
don't get to be with my friends.
With Sara. I told her I don't
mind. Sara begged me to find a

way to go to the beach with her and her friends. Our friends. She said she would stay, but I insisted she go. I miss her, though. I miss holding her. It's only a week, but it feels like an eternity without her.

CHAPTER 8

Lenox

I T'S BEEN THREE WEEKS OF searching. Searching for a girl who may or may not tell me to eat shit when I find her. Sammy and I tried googling every place that had a lost and found program. I'm not sure if we used the wrong search words, but we hit a dead end every time.

Then this morning, as if a switch was flipped on, I remembered her mentioning something about where she found my journal. I scrolled through email after email until I finally found what I was looking for. Faulk Central Library.

It's still a long shot. There isn't a real plan. My only strategy is to walk in and hope the librarian is willing to provide me with the information I need to find this girl. Asking for the name of the place that picks through their lost and found isn't violating any privacy laws.

I'll ask, say my thanks, and leave. Simple.

I stare through the glass doors, noticing the rows of books cases and tables, recalling the last time I was here. I sat there, turning the pages of my journal, looking for something I had written that might convince Sara to take me back. Barely awake, running on only a few hours of sleep. Desperate. Broken. Pathetic.

My God. I never want to be there again. Be that person again.

Suddenly, I turn away from the building and begin walking toward the corner of the intersection. I stare at the crosswalk, waiting for it to change, allowing me to leave this behind me. Who cares if she has my journal? What does it matter? Apparently, she's given up, because it's been three weeks since she's emailed me. She's a stranger. None of it matters. The emails. The feelings she stirred in me. I don't want that...or do I?

The light changes and the walk signal begins to flash, signaling to me that it's safe to walk across the street. It's safe. Is it? I turn and look back at the library. *Safe. Safe. Safe*, repeats in my mind to the tempo of my heart.

Closing my eyes, I take a breath and look back at the crosswalk sign. It's flashing orange now...3...2...1.

I missed my chance. Or did I?

What are you doing? I think to myself. That's just it. I have no idea what I'm doing. Ever since TC emailed her way into my life, a flame was lit in me. A flame I can't seem to tamp out no matter what I do.

Indeed, what could this hurt? *You. It could hurt you,* my mind whispers. I shake the thought away.

Ignoring my unease, I walk to the glass doors and pull them open, directing my attention to the checkout desk.

As I approach, a loud thump echoes through the quietness of the library. I watch as the woman working behind the counter rushes around the desk toward the sound. Turning my attention to the direction she is going, I stop instantly. A girl—no, a woman—whispering curse words repeatedly under her breath is turning a box over from its side. Her dark blonde hair touched with golden highlights from the sun is hanging around her face. She begins picking up items and tossing them into the box. I watch as the librarian rushes up and squats down to assist her.

She begins reassuring the woman in a whisper. "Oh, Tessa, don't worry about it."

Tessa. My heart skips a beat. Tessa.

I step back behind a bookshelf. I know I should be ashamed for eavesdropping, but I can't help myself. I have to be sure it's her. Something is telling me it's her. What are the odds? I listen. I wait. My heart beats out of my chest.

A tinkle of laughter carries its way over to me.

"I don't know what's wrong with me today, Marylou. It seems like I just can't move without dropping or spilling something. I should never be allowed out in public," she jokes quietly.

"Don't be silly," the woman I now know as Marylou replies.

I peer through the books, watching them place the items back in the box, then carry it over to the desk. I remain frozen in my hiding place listening. Watching.

"So, how did your blind date go Chad set you up on a few weeks ago?" Marylou asks her.

Her back is to me. From behind, I can tell she is slender. The skirt she is wearing flares out a little above the knee, but showing enough of her legs for me to know they are long and tone. A runner possibly. She is wearing a cardigan sweater the color of leaves in spring and I wonder what color her eyes might be.

Shaking her head slightly, she replies, "I've given up on romance." She pauses before continuing, "I'm not sure it exists anymore." She releases a quiet sigh. "I know I sound cynical, but it seems the idea of true love is nonexistent. People don't write love letters anymore or send flowers. There aren't any impromptu unexpected gestures of love. Maybe I'm just setting myself up for disappointment...my expectations are too high. I don't know."

The way her voice sounds catches my attention. The words leaving her lips causing my heart to tighten in my chest. I want to say no. I want to say she is wrong yet I can't. I remain silent. Paralyzed. A part of me understands. I'm not sure it exists either.

She laughs, but it's a sad laugh. I've never hated the sound so much. It seems wrong coming from her.

Feeling out of my element, I suck in a deep breath. I haven't even met her, yet I understand her. I don't know her, but I want to know her. I want to change her mind about love. Even more than that, I want her to change mine.

Turning my attention back to Tessa and the librarian, I hear them say their goodbyes. She walks away and briefly looks back lifting her hand to push the loose strands of hair in her eyes behind her ear. The look on her face makes me think she forgot something. Her gaze roams over the room for only a moment before turning once more and walking out the door. She's gone. I just let her walk away.

What would I have said anyway?

Rolling my shoulders, I turn, slumping against the bookcase. Pull it together. I know her name. I just need to locate where I can find her.

Noticing Marylou is still standing behind the desk, I walk over, clearing my throat before speaking.

"Excuse me," I say.

Looking up, she gives me a warm smile. "Hello. How may I help you?"

How may she help me? Speak, Lenox. She just continues to smile. Waiting.

Finally, I smile politely back. "Uh...yeah...yes...I'm wondering if you can tell me where the young lady you were just speaking to works?"

Her smile falters a little, so I continue.

"It's just that I noticed she takes your lost and found items. I'm interested in setting up a similar arrangement." I sound like an idiot.

She watches me. Her eyes are roaming my face. Then, as if she decides I'm harmless, she answers, "I'm assuming you mean Tessa. She works for Hands of Hope. It's the local homeless shelter. The lost and found program is something she started a year or so ago. The program is designed to help provide items for the homeless men and women in our city so they can get their lives back. It is a pretty fantastic idea Tessa came up with. She's pretty amazing."

A homeless shelter. Tessa.

I lock my gaze with hers. "Yeah, she sounds like it. Thank you for the information." I reach my hand across the counter, and she takes it in a gentle handshake. "I'll get in contact with her...them."

As I back away, she gives me a knowing smile.

"Thanks again," I stutter out.

Quickly, I make my way out of the library and onto the street again, gasping for air like I was holding my breath the entire time.

I've searched for her for three weeks, and it isn't until this moment that I think about why. Our exchanges were brief and most of the time unfriendly, but I just felt something. Something that scares me, but I'm not sure I should fear it.

Who made her stop believing in love?

A homeless shelter. Dealing with people lost in this world. Only someone with a huge heart could do what she does.

This being said, how does a person with this kind of heart not believe that true love exists anymore.

And how do I change her mind?

June 16, 2008

It's summer. Freshman year down and we made it. Sara and I survived our first year of college. We still have our love. We still have our hope. We still have one another. Sara seems to believe again, too. I'm glad the doubt doesn't show in her eyes any longer. I told her we would endure and we will. I'll keep on loving her forever. Nothing could ever change how I feel about her.

CHAPTER 9

Lenox

"SO WHAT YOU'RE TELLING ME is you found her and said nothing. You just watched her…from behind a bookcase, and said nothing." Sammy paces in front of me, running his hand through his hair. "Dude, you're a fucking creeper! Even I'm a little frightened of you."

I don't look up right away. He waits for me to say something. Do something.

"Screw you, Sam," I finally reply, glancing up at him. "It wasn't …isn't like that."

He laughs. "Well, maybe you can explain what it's like because from where I'm standing that is exactly what it sounds like. Nox… you stood behind a bookcase, listened to her conversation, and watched her without ever letting her know you were there. It's major pervert material."

"You don't get it, Sammy. It wasn't the right time. You didn't see her. Hear her."

Taking a seat next to me on the couch, he slaps his hand on my shoulder, slightly knocking me forward.

"Then what's your plan? I know you well enough to know you have something going on in that head of yours where this girl is concerned."

Leaning back, I allow my head to fall against the back of the couch, looking up at the ceiling.

"I'm not entirely sure yet, but I can promise you that it won't be illegal or creepy. Even though sitting outside her house in my white creeper van sounds pretty tempting," I joke back.

I told him I don't know what I'm going to do about this whole situation with Tessa, but if I'm honest, I know what I'm going to do. I just hope it works.

Getting up, Sammy walks toward the door.

"As much as I enjoy sitting here chatting with you about some chick you're stalking, I gotta get to work. Later."

Shaking my head at his comment, I lift my hand in a small salute as I stand up. "Later."

I hear the door open and begin to shut before Sam throws in one last comment.

"Oh and Nox?" Sammy says from the doorway.

Facing him, I respond. "Yeah?"

"I'm glad you found her even if you were too chicken shit to talk to her."

The door quickly shuts behind him before I can even say anything. He's such an asshole.

It's strange. I feel a little queasy as I put pen to paper. Hesitating, my mind wanders into the past for a moment. This is the first time in what seems like an eternity I've written in this way. From the heart. From a place of vulnerability.

My last journal entry had two words and was incomplete. I had nothing left to say so I got up, walked out of the library, leaving my journal. It's those lack of words and heartbreak that led me to this moment.

This exact moment. What do I say to this girl…in this moment?

How do I approach this? She doesn't believe in true love or romance. I have to prove her wrong, yet I question if I believe in it myself anymore.

That burning sensation in my chest that appears when that thought crosses my mind, flares.

I need to do this right. Obviously, this isn't a love letter, but it will be a start.

Hopefully, it will be a start of something that has been missing from her life…and from mine.

Once again, I find myself standing outside of a building downtown. Debating on whether or not I want to walk through two doors, knowing the consequence of this simple action will change everything.

Opening myself up to the possibility to feel something again, when I finally feel whole.

Taking a deep breath, I place one foot in front of the other, reaching my hand out to the steel handle of the door to pull it open. The handle is cold; the door is heavy. When I enter, there is a low buzzing of voices echoing throughout the room. People are moving busily about the room. Some are sitting together while one takes notes and the other talks.

A large desk is directly in front of me as I walk farther into the big open space. At first, it appears that no one is there until I take a closer look and realize a tiny older woman is sitting behind the desk. Her head full of gray hair peeking just over the top.

When I finally reach the desk, the elderly lady looks up at me with a friendly smile.

"Hello, sweetie. I'm Sue. How may we help you today?" she inquires in a gentle, pleasant manner.

I give her a genuine smile.

"Hi, Sue. I'm wondering if I could leave something for Tessa." I figure I will keep it casual as if it isn't unusual for me to be here, asking about Tessa.

Her grin widens as her eyes roam over my face. Why does that keep happening when I mention Tessa to these ladies? It's beginning to make me a little self-conscious.

"Absolutely, but you can give it to her yourself. She's in her office. It's directly down that hall to your left, second door on the right," she explains. "Wait…no…no, that's not right. She's not in her office. It's Thursday. Tessa and Chad always have a meeting at this time on Thursdays."

I want to laugh at her mumbling. Her manner is kind yet scattered. She's not here. Tessa is at a meeting. Maybe I could leave it on her desk instead of handing it off to Sue.

"Sue, do you think I could just drop this on Tessa's desk instead?" I request. I give her another warm smile, hoping to charm her enough to allow it.

She begins stammering again. "Well, sure. Just go on back and leave it."

Before she realizes it might not be a good idea to let a stranger in Tessa's office, I wave my thanks to her and head to Tessa's office. I pass a woman and a child; who I can only assume is her daughter. The little girl looks directly at me; I recognize the uncertainty she is feeling in her eyes. I see it every week in the young boys I mentor at the boys club. I was that boy once myself. I move my lips into a small smile to let her know I see her. She instantly returns it.

When I reach the hallway, I glance behind me to make sure no one is following me. Reaching the second door on the right, I read the name plaque with her name. I recite her name out loud. "Tessa Collins." *TC. Tessa Collins.*

Turning the knob of the door to her office, I walk through, looking around.

Sitting on a shelf behind her desk is a single framed photo, so I walk closer to get a better look. The photo is an older couple, most likely her parents, they're smiling at one another. Their arms wrapped around the other's shoulders. The woman in the photo has the same golden locks, but it barely reaches her shoulders. The man is tall with dark hair. I turn back to her desk, realizing that I need to hurry since I'm unsure of when she'll be back.

Pivoting toward her desk, I place the letter up against her computer monitor; her name scrawled across the front.

I reach for it, contemplating taking it back. Maybe I should forget this whole idea.

No. No, I'm doing it. There's no turning back; I'm going to write these letters to Tessa and somehow prove to her that romance still exists.

January 26, 2009

Sara is mad at me. We've fought before, but this time seems different. She can't seem to believe we'll make it through. I asked her what she wanted, and she said she didn't know. I love her. She says she loves me. Love can be hard. This is our hard part. I'll never stop believing.

CHAPTER 10

TESSA

FALLING INTO THE CHAIR AT my desk, I release a heavy sigh. What a day. Thursdays are always full of meetings. Long, drawn-out, tiring meetings. Some weeks I don't even have time to breathe.

Closing my eyes, I let my head rest against the back of my chair as my mind runs through my to-do list. So much to do. So little time. It's the story of my life.

I just need to get up and call it a day. Go home. Pour a glass of wine. Relax.

I open my eyes, reaching over for my mouse to shut down for the day. Leaning against my monitor is an envelope with my name written across the front. My heart stops beating. My ability to breathe gone. That handwriting. Unease churns in my stomach. What the hell?

Slowly, I reach my shaking hand for the envelope, hovering over it for a second, debating if I even want to touch it. I have to open it. There isn't a choice.

Picking it up, I grab my letter opener and slice it open. My hands are quivering even harder at the prospect of what's inside. I can't wrap my mind around how this is possible, but I know it's him. I would recognize his handwriting anywhere.

I pull the sheet of paper from the envelope and try to unfold it steadily.

Taking a deep breath, I allow my eyes to roam over the words.

Tessa,

I'm sure you're confused right now. So am I. For some reason, that doesn't matter. As I write this letter, I wonder if you will recognize the writing. Maybe it looks familiar, and you can't place it. Or maybe you instantly realize you've seen my handwriting, and you're shocked that I'm writing to you. It's just there are things I need to say...to you.

We don't know one another. You know my thoughts, but you don't know me. I know you think you know me from the words written in my journal, or maybe from the harshness of my emails. But you don't. You don't know the real me at all. Just like I don't know the real you.

I know this is going to sound crazy, but I looked for you. It was something I felt I needed to do. You intrigued me. Every snarky remark. Every time you made it clear you didn't believe I wrote those words, the curiosity grew within me. It grew so big that I couldn't think of anything else. I'm not entirely sure why you never believed me, but I'm glad you didn't because if you had believed me, then I never would have searched for the fascinating girl from the emails. I needed to find you.

And I did. I found you just like you found my journal. (Yes, it's my journal.)

I saw you. I heard you, and this is what I realized. You don't want to throw away my journal, and I don't want you to throw away your belief in romance.

Don't you see, Tessa? I believed in love too, before I didn't. I believed in the romantic and genuine kind of love. Until I didn't.

I thought I never wanted to believe again. To be vulnerable to the possibility of hurt. I thought I felt this way until I heard your sweet voice say you didn't believe it existed anymore either. It was at that moment I knew I wanted to prove to you that you are wrong. To prove that I'm wrong. To show you romance does exist.

I knew I couldn't let that happen, and I needed a plan. So here it is, I'm going to write to you. Sure, I may not love you, but knowing what I know about you, I like you a whole hell of a lot.

So that's it. I'm going to write "like" letters to you so I can prove romance hasn't died. To convince you. And maybe, just maybe I will convince myself, too.

Yours in admiration.

I read it over and over. I read it until my eyes blur. I attempt to read it until the shaking stops, but I'm not sure it ever will.

Finally, I fold the letter, pick up my belongings, and walk toward the front desk. Sue must have seen him.

As I approach, Sue is hanging up the phone and looks up at me. "Hello, Tessa. Are you leaving for the day?"

"Hi, Sue, yes, but I wanted to ask you something first."

"Of course. Oh, did you talk to your friend? The handsome young man who was asking for you earlier?" she asks in her usual rushed fashion.

Well, she beat me to it. Handsome? My friend?

"Was he handsome? I mean, I don't think I would say he is my friend. Did he say we were friends?" I stumble over my words. My heart is still racing from the words written in the letter left on my desk. I just don't understand why he's doing this?

Maybe he's crazy. Great, it would be just my luck to get mixed up with a crazy yet extremely literate guy.

"Well, come to think of it, I don't think he ever said he knew you. I just assumed because he asked for you by name and he was very handsome," she says with a slightly dreamy look in her eyes before continuing to ramble, That's twice now she mentioned he's handsome. "He looked as if he spends time in the gym. Very active. A little rugged..." She looks up at me. "He had short, messy hair. Yes, definitely handsome. Although, he had those tattoos. Why you young people think you need to cover your body in art is beyond me."

For someone so senile, Sue certainly can remember details and paint quite the picture.

I'm only more intrigued, but nope. I can't allow this.

Sue looks up at me again. "Is he not your friend? Because I was certain, he knew you."

"Uh, well, no, he isn't my friend, but..." I don't even get to finish.

"Oh my word, Tessa! I'm so sorry!" Sue exclaims, placing her small wrinkly hand over her heart in her typical dramatic fashion.

"No worries, Sue. It's fine," I reassure her. "See you tomorrow."

Turning to walk away, I pause mid-step.

"Sue, did he happen to mention his name?" I inquire, trying to appear more casual than I feel on the inside.

"Well, honey, now that you mention it, he didn't," she replies. "Or did he?" She laughs. "You know this mind of mine. It remembers what it wants."

"Oh, okay," I say, trying to hide my disappointment. "Thanks again. See you tomorrow."

I walk through the front doors, feeling more exhausted...more confused than ever.

"I've read it to you three times, Chad; I doubt a fourth time will provide any further insight into what this guy is trying to do," I stated, a sigh escaping my lips.

Chad and I have been on the phone for the last forty-five minutes trying to determine this mystery guy's intentions.

"Sweetie, I realized that a long time ago. I'm just in love with this letter," Chad explains. "It may be simple...and strange, but it's also romantic. And did I mention strange."

"It is strange!" I reiterate a little too enthusiastically. "I mean, who writes a letter like this? He still didn't leave his name."

"Well, you do know his email and address, Buttercup, you could just email him, or better yet go to his house," he suggests as if it's just that simple.

"No way! I can't do that because...because...well, I just can't do it. I think it's best I just ignore him because he's toying with me. Lying asshole is using me for entertainment, and I'm not falling into his trap," I declare.

I can picture his eyes rolling as he says, "Okay, whatever you say. We'll just forget about mystery letter boy and move onto the paramount date tonight boy. What are you wearing?"

Now I'm rolling my eyes. I'm not sure why I continue to allow Chad to set me up on these blind dates. Disasters. Every single one.

"I don't know," I reply, knowing as soon as the thought leaves my lips I will receive a lecture.

"You don't know! Tes, you are utterly hopeless. Why do I keep trying if you don't make any attempt to try yourself?" he scolds in his typical Chad manner.

"It's not that I don't try, but it's not like any of these have worked out so well in the past. It'll be fine."

"Yes, I'm sure it will. I think this one could be the one," he says, hope curling around his words.

I can't help myself when I laugh at his comment. He says this every time, yet it's never been the one. Is there even such a thing as "the one"? As soon as the thought enters my mind, I think of the letter and his words. His declaration to change my mind. *I'm going to write "like" letters to you so I can prove romance hasn't died. To convince you. And maybe...just maybe I will convince myself, too. I* would be lying if I said I didn't feel an ounce of hope that he will be able to convince me.

───────────────

I stare across the table at my date. I wonder if they would dismiss the charges against me if I stab this fork into his hand. Has anyone ever received life in prison for doing something like that? I don't want to kill him. I just want to hurt him. And his hand. The hand that has misbehaved and crossed lines this entire date.

What kind of person thinks it's okay to pick food off of their date's plate? A first date! A blind first date! I feel my blood pressure rising again. Those are my damn fries.

And as if that weren't bad enough, 'grabby' Grant then proceeded to reach under the table and try to cop a feel. His greasy fingers sweeping across my thigh. I almost went GI Jane on his ass. Instead, I abruptly declared a need to use the ladies room and stood up, his hand dropping from my knee.

"Hello. Tessa, come back to us," His voice breaks into my thoughts. I look up at him blinking. The fork still firmly in my grip. When he knows he has my attention, he continues, "Did you want dessert?"

I blink again. Dessert? Maybe some sugar will calm me down. I doubt this night could get worse.

"Sure, I would love dessert," I finally respond. "The crème Brulee sounds delicious,"

I smile at the waitress, who looks awkwardly between me and my date.

He smiles at her and orders. "I'll have the chocolate mousse. Also, can you split the check?"

My jaw drops. The grip on the fork tightens. And all I can think is romance is most definitely dead.

September 9, 2009

Sara is worried our class schedules will interfere with our time
together. She says she can't see
how it will work. Again, I'm reassuring her we'll be okay. We
are going to school to better our
future. I reminded her it's our
future, and although our schedule is a bit tight this semester,
we can make it through any-

thing. I asked her if she loved
me and she said yes. I told her
that our love is all that matters.

CHAPTER II

TESSA

I WEAVE THE ENVELOPE BETWEEN my fingers, trying to decide if I want to open it. That is the question: do I want to open it? I can't understand the fear I felt when I saw a letter once again propped up against my computer monitor on my desk.

It's been a week since he left the first message for me. I was just beginning to forget about this whole mission to prove romance still exists then I walk into my office after my meetings and there it was sitting on my desk.

Immediately, I called the front desk to ask Sue about it. She had no idea what I was even talking about and said she hadn't seen the gentleman from last week.

How did he do it? Because he was here. In my office. He was in this room, and I have no idea what he looks like or who he is. I feel like this should frighten me, but oddly it doesn't. It makes me feel something I can't explain.

Taking a deep breath, I hold it out in front of me. I stare at every loop in the letters of my name, neatly written across the front then I slip the letter out and unfold it slowly.

Tessa,

   A week has gone by, and I've thought of you every day. I've spent...extended periods of time distracted by thoughts of what your reaction to my first letter may have been. I imagine you were shocked and confused. Maybe a little taken aback by what I'm proposing. Then I wondered if you thought about emailing me. If you considered coming to my house. You did neither of those things and honestly, I'm glad. I hope it means you accept my challenge.

   Do you accept my challenge, Tessa? Do you want to believe in romance? In true love again? Did you ever believe?

   Let me do this. Let this happen. Answer the questions I ask you in these letters.

   Because guess what? For romance to live and work, for it to thrive and blossom into its full beauty, it takes two people, not just one. If you learn to believe, then I think maybe I will believe again, too.

   Let's start out simple. What is your favorite color? Your favorite song?

   Find a way to let me know.

Just as I did with the first letter, I read his words over and over. My heart is beating more rapidly each time. Two letters. Only two letters and I'm in knots. I don't understand why he's doing this.

   I don't understand what all of this means. Am I brave enough to find out?

   I drum my fingers against the tabletop as my date talks on his cell phone across from me. He has been on the phone for fifteen minutes...this time. This is the third phone call he's taken since we arrived at the restaurant an hour ago.

Wasn't it just last week I swore off blind dates? God, I hate Chad.

"Yeah...yeah...okay...sure...uh huh...sure. Sounds great. I'll see you tomorrow," he says into his phone.

I stop drumming my fingers. He's finally getting off the phone. I sit up straight giving him my attention as he hangs up the phone.

"So, dollface, do you wanna order?" he asks me, showing me his recently bleached teeth. Oh my God, did he just wink at me? No. Just no. "Sorry about the phone calls; it's called life when you're important."

I turn my head to hide my rolling eyes.

Why me? Ugh. No pity parties. Can I feel sorry for myself when I agree to be setup with these guys? No, I can't, but I can hate Chad though for having such horrible taste. I look up to my date. He's smiling as he looks through his phone. Yep. I hate Chad.

Our waiter walks up to our table, greeting us once again with an expectant look. He wants us to order. I'm sure the forty-five minutes we've been sitting at his table without ordering are cutting into his tips. Oh God, he's going to spit in our food.

Quickly, I begin to apologize. "I'm so sorry we've been sitting here for so long without ordering. I think we're ready now." If I'm apologetic and polite, then maybe he'll leave his revenge spit out of my food.

"Yeah, what she said," my date contributes without looking up from his phone. "Can you get us two ribeyes and side salads with ranch dressing? Thanks, man." He orders for me and dismisses the waiter without ever looking up at us.

My mouth falls open. I hate steak. I hate ranch dressing even more. My eyes flash to the waiter, who is turning on his heels, rolling his eyes, a disgusted look on his face. My God, he is totally spitting in our food.

Quickly, my hand darts out and wraps around our waiter's wrist. "I'm sorry, but I'd like to order something else," I say, my voice dripping with frustration, I release his arm. "I'd much rather have the grilled chicken and steamed veggies. Thank you." Pushing my annoyance with my date, I smile at the young guy. He returns my smile and I can see a bit of pity in his eyes. "Sure, I'll have that right out to you."

"So, dollface, I'm treating you to a nice dinner and my company. What are you doing for me?" His words pull my attention back to him and the arrogant smirk on his face. He really can't be this clueless.

Someone kill me now.

* * *

Sitting in my car, staring at his front door, I wonder why I'm here. No, wait. That's a lie. I know exactly why I'm here.

I want to believe. I want to accept his challenge. I want to see where this is going and just how far he'll take it. Although, after the date I just walked out on I'm not sure why I would even want to risk the possibility of disappointment.

All of the lights are off in the house. He doesn't appear to be home—exactly what I was hoping.

Glancing in the rear-view mirror, I give myself a pep talk. "You can do this! You want to do this! Take a risk!" I'm sure I look crazy yelling at my reflection, all alone in my car.

I can do this.

Grabbing the handle of the door, I throw it open and hop out. I dash across the street and up onto the porch. It would be just my luck if he pulled up while I'm here. While the idea of actually seeing him in person is appealing, I'm not ready for this little charade to end.

I don't even bother knocking; I press the pink sticky note on the chipped, painted blue door. I don't miss the irony that this same action is how this all began. My heart beat speeds up in anticipation of his next letter. I'm already starting to feel it, that spark of hope.

The only problem is, I don't have a clue what I wish to happen.

April 4, 2010

Another semester is almost over. It has been rough, but Sara and I are still in love. We made new promises last night. Promises to keep loving one another. Promises to hold on because we're worth it. We'll always keep holding on. Forever. I'll hold on to Sara as long as she lets me. Sara is still my everything. Nearly four years and she's still everything I want.

CHAPTER 12

Lenox

I SEE IT BEFORE I even reach the top porch step. The bright pink stands out against the blue of the door. She was here. I look around me like she might still be here even though I know she isn't.

She found a way to answer me. With a pink sticky note. This means something. No, not something—it means everything. Another crack forms in the armor I placed over my heart.

Without looking at it, I pull the pink note from the door and walk into the house.

I'm just not ready to read it. Maybe it says for me to leave her alone. Maybe she doesn't want to do this. Maybe she does. I'm not sure what scares me more. Until this moment, I don't think I realized just how much I want this whole thing to work. Not just for her, but for me.

I want to believe in love again.

I throw my bag on the couch as I walk by and head to my room. With each step I take, the knot in my stomach tightens. Once in my room, I walk to my desk and switch on the light. Taking a seat, I press the note flat against the desk, my hand covering it. This is it.

Slowly, I move my hand, letting my gaze roam over the words. A slow smile forms on my mouth.

> FAVORITE COLOR:
> YELLOW. NOT JUST ANY YELLOW,
> BUT BUTTER YELLOW.
> FAVORITE SONG:
> "CALL CALL CALL" BY WILL JOHNSON
> I LOVE WORDS IN ALL FORMS. LYRICS.
> BOOKS. POEMS. YOU'VE CAUGHT MY
> ATTENTION. I HOPE YOU KNOW WHAT
> YOU'RE DOING. MY GOD, I HOPE
> I KNOW WHAT I'M DOING.
> RELUCTANTLY,
> TESSA

Short, sweet, and to the point. She answered my questions and gave me a little more. I glance across the room to my reflection in the mirror hanging on the wall. The look in my eyes is telling me what my mind already knows. I have no idea what I'm doing, but I know I can't stop now.

"So tell me what's new in your life."

She leans forward, placing her elbows on the table in front of her, giving me that motherly look I've seen for years. The one that tells me she knows something is going on in my life but wants me to open up without her needing to pry too much.

"Not much," I reply nonchalantly. I figure I'll make her work a little for the answer she's seeking.

"Lenox Evan Malone, don't make me beg for information," she demands with exasperation. Uh oh, she means business. She used all three of my names. It would be scary if it were any other mother than Kristin Malone.

Laughing on the inside, I mirror her, placing my elbows on the table and fix a serious look on my face.

"What do you know and who have you been talking to?"

I see the guilty look cross her features briefly.

"I'm your mother, so I don't have to explain myself," she grins. "If you must know, I ran into Sammy, and he may or may not have mentioned that you met someone." She looks hopeful. My mom was there every step of the way through my relationship ups and downs with Sara. I think she worries too much.

"Figures. Damn, Sammy can't keep his mouth shut." Taking a drink of my iced tea, I try to think how I'll explain this to her. I barely understand what I'm doing. "Mom, look, I haven't exactly met someone."

"What does that even mean, Lenox?" she asks, a slightly confused look on her face. "Either you have, or you haven't, and Sammy seems to think you have, and he appeared to believe you've fallen for someone."

"Whoa, that's a big stretch. First, don't listen to Sammy. He exaggerates and is making more of this than it is. Second, I haven't actually met her." I'm going to need to explain before she lets her imagination run wild.

As much as my mom tries to stay out of my business most of the time, my relationships with the opposite sex are a bit touchy. I know she's my mom, and she's only worried about me

she worries too much.

"I can see that you're worried, but you shoulu.

is, Mom, I haven't exactly met this girl, but I want tu

We're communicating, but I'm going about this in a different wa

don't know what is happening exactly, but I won't get hurt, so you can stop worrying." I reach my hand out and place it over hers. "I promise. Plus, I'm nearly twenty-seven years old, and I'm pretty sure there have been guys my age who've had far more broken hearts than me. I'll be fine. Okay?"

"Fine, but don't forget I'm your mother, and I don't like seeing you hurt." She gives me that half smile that lets me know she's still worried, but will let this go for now. "Now, let's order because I'm starving."

It's just like her to let things go so quickly. It was always just the two of us, she held on tight when she needed, but gave me room to fall so I could learn to pick myself back up. Kristin Malone never had it easy, but she always worked hard and did everything on her own. I guess that's what she has always wanted for me.

"Me, too. Three days of ramen noodles isn't doing it for me anymore."

"Lenox, I taught you to cook, so utilize the skill. I'm not going to feel sorry for you when it's your choice to live off ramen noodles. As you pointed out, you're twenty-seven years old; your college days are over. Not to mention, ramen noodles never impressed a girl that I know of," she scolds playfully. "Now, feed your mother."

Picking up her menu, she scans it quickly. I've never known her to order anything other than the macaroni and cheese; she's a creature of habit.

"I don't even know why you bother looking at that thing. You know you're not going to try something different," I tease, and she ignores me.

I may not always be lucky in love, but I'll be damned if I didn't win the mom lotto.

"Dude, you've gotta quit telling my mom shit. She has too many other things to worry about than my love life," I insist as I walk down the street to the car to go to lunch.

"Sorry, man, but she puts a spell on me," he replies without guilt.

I turn and punch him in the arm.

"What the hell?" he shouts in pain as he grabs his left arm with his right hand.

"You're talking about my mom."

"I'm not blind; she's hot."

"Seriously, Sammy. I'm going to kill you."

"She asked so what was I supposed to do? Lie to her?" Sammy responds as he reaches over and rubs his arm again.

"You didn't need to lie. You just could've left the part about Tessa out. I don't know what's even happening with this whole thing, and now my mom is already worrying that I'll have my heart broken," I tell him.

"Nox, my lips are sealed, but I'm kind of worried myself. What are you doing?" He stops walking, and I have to turn back to look at him. "You're writing this girl love letters and sneaking them into her work to give them to her. Why don't you just talk to her? Introduce yourself and ask her out or don't ask her out. You have nothing to prove. I get that you're over Sara, but you don't have to do this whole thing with this girl."

"Damn it, Sam! This isn't about Sara, and I do have to do this with this girl. Even if I'm not sure why or where this will all lead, I know I'm doing what I need to do."

He stares at me, his eyes searching my face for something, then shrugs his shoulders before saying, "If you say so, man."

November 15, 2010

Thanksgiving break begins to-morrow. Mom has everything planned. I can't wait to see her and spend time with her. Sara will come over when she gets back from her grandmother's house. Thanksgiving will be just about mom and me. The only other woman I love as much as Sara. The woman who taught me how to love. I'm so thankful for both of them. They're all I need. Okay, maybe I need Sammy, too. I won't ever tell him that, though.

CHAPTER 13

Lenox

A S MY FEET POUND THE pavement, my mind drifts to the conversations I had with my mom and Sammy over the last couple of days. Their concerns and questions are playing over and over in my mind with every stride.

My mom is worried I'm going to get hurt. Sammy wants to know what I'm doing. The answer is I have no idea.

If I'm really honest, these letters are a way for me to avoid getting too close. A way to keep myself at a distance because after Sara, I never want to be vulnerable again. But, why would this make me vulnerable? Maybe I need to take this chance because there is one thing I'm sure about when it comes to this whole crazy situation; I want to know Tessa.

Lengthening my stride, I round the street corner toward my house. Sweat is dripping down my face as I push myself harder. My heart rate is picking up with each stride and from the thoughts racing through my mind. I'll never outrun these anxieties over opening up to the possibility of finding myself broken again.

I know what I want, and sometimes, you have to push through your fears to find what makes you happy. Do I know if Tessa is that happiness? No, but I'm not willing to let that pass by me.

Sammy is right. I need to talk to her. Not just through letters, but in person. It's possible to show her romance exists without hiding behind these letters. Isn't it more romantic to take the risk?

I slow to a stop on my front lawn, bending at the waist, hands on my knees. Trying to catch my breath, I make up my mind. I'm going to write her a letter and propose we meet. I'm not sure she'll say yes, but I have to try.

Damn it; I hate when Sammy is right.

Tessa,

Yellow? I find it interesting since yellow is never a person's favorite color. You got me thinking about the color yellow. I tried to think of things I love that are yellow. Lemons. I like lemons. In my tea. Lemon cake. Lemon Piccata. I guess those things aren't the color yellow, but in a way they represent them. I like dandelions. They remind me of when I was a kid and how I would pick them for my mom. Yellow is pretty great if you think about it. It represents happy things. Are you happy? It makes me wonder what your favorite color says about you. I want to find out if it means anything at all.

Will Johnson, huh? A guy off the radar in a way, but should be on everyone's playlist. I have to admit I fell a little bit in love with you when I read that your favorite song is "Call Call Call" by Will Johnson. And maybe a little more in love with the idea that you even know who Will Johnson is. People who know him, love him. People who don't are missing out.

Which leads me to what I want to say next. I don't want to miss out on knowing you. I've been thinking a lot about these letters and the idea that I want to prove to you romance still exist. I can't answer why I need you to believe in romance, but I do. I realize I need to believe again, too. More importantly, I want to feel again.

Here is what I'm proposing: Let's meet. In person. Face to face.

Isn't there something romantic about talking and getting to know one another in person? Life is one big game of chance. We have a choice in how we play it. I'm drawn to you, and I want to find out why. I want to experience why you were drawn to me. I can only conclude that you read something in my journal that interests you. You said it yourself, I captured your attention, and you've definitely captured mine.

So agree to meet me. I'll leave it to you to name the place and time. Take a chance on a possibility of something you least expected.

With admiration.

PS. The sticky note was a nice touch. Some might say, romantic.

Letter in my pocket, I jog down the sidewalk toward the Hands of Hope building. I still have thirty minutes left in the window of time Tessa's away from her office. I've been trying to get used to the idea that I've suggested we meet.

It may seem simple, but I feel like I need to prepare myself mentally. It's the reason I don't just walk into her office when she is there and introduce myself. I need to be ready. Maybe I'm overthinking it all, but as much as I know it's the right thing to do; I'm not completely prepared.

Giving her this letter puts the ball in her court. What if she doesn't want to meet me? I'm just leaving it up to her, not to mention I don't want to blindside her by just walking into her life like I belong there.

As I approach the corner of the building, I think to myself; we'll find out what fate has in store for us.

And that's when fate let me know just what that might be.

January 17, 2011

The holidays are over. School is starting again, and life keeps going. I told Sara that's exactly what we have to do. We have to keep looking forward because that's where our future is. We are still together every moment we aren't in class or working. I'm still just as in love with her as I've ever been.

CHAPTER 14

TESSA

A N ARM FULL OF FILES, I race to Java Joe's for a cup of coffee, the much-needed caffeine before I have to be back at the office for a quick meeting then another dreaded date. Why do I keep punishing myself? It's a wonder Chad, and I are still friends.

Picking up the pace, I rush around the corner of the building. Suddenly, my files are flying in the air, and I'm stumbling to keep from falling. A small squeal is echoing through the air. A hand firmly wraps around my wrist and pulls me forward.

"Holy shit, I'm sorry," a deep, soothing voice says.

I turn my face to the stranger, and the words I was about to say are lost. Handsome, kind eyes are suddenly looking at me with a guarded familiarity that's creating a tingling sensation in the center of my chest.

I watch him squat down, picking up my files while keeping his eyes trained on my face. I don't move. A crooked smile appears on his face, and suddenly, words pour out of my mouth.

"Oh, I'm just standing here while you pick up my stuff. I wasn't paying attention, so don't apologize." I reach out and take the files he is now extending toward me.

"I wasn't exactly paying attention either," he admits.

I laugh. "Yes, well it seems both of us want to take the blame."

"It seems so," he agrees.

He's staring at me. The look is sending a shiver down my spine. It's like he's trying to tell me something, but I don't understand what it could be.

"The ocean," he states.

Confused, I look around before saying, "Excuse, me?"

"Your eyes. They're the color of the sea."

There's that fluttering again, moving around in my stomach. I can feel the heat moving through me, staining my skin a rosy shade of pink.

Pushing a few strands of hair behind my ear, I can think of nothing else to say but, "Oh."

"I know this is going to sound strange, but can I buy you a cup of coffee or something?" He widens his smile; it's hopeful, and that does something to my heart.

Yes, it is weird since we just met, sort of. I don't even know his name. He is handsome. Even though he has a beard, I can see his chiseled jawline. His eyes shine with kindness. I shouldn't. But, then again, I was already on my way to grab a coffee, so what would it hurt for me to allow him to buy me a cup? What would Chad do? Wait. That's a dumb question; Chad would already be walking away with him. Come on, Tessa. Do it. Live a little. This wouldn't be any different than all of the dates you've been going on, but of course, this isn't a date. Holy hell, he's still staring at me, waiting for an answer.

"Sure, why not? I was just on my way to grab a cup of coffee anyway," I reply, trying to sound nonchalant when my nerves are rattled.

A surprised look crosses his features and quickly disappears.

"Great…great. Uh, shall we?" He stutters out.

"Sure, but first things first," I say before reaching my hand out to him. "I'm Tessa Collins, nice to meet you."

He looks down at my hand and then back up to my face.

Taking my hand in his, he introduces himself. "Nice to meet you, Tessa. I'm Lenox. Lenox Malone.

Our hands linger between us, wrapped around one another. Lenox Malone. I like the way his name sounds. The way he's looking at me. I wonder what else I will like about him.

───────────────

With every glance, I see a spark in his eyes flare. A familiarity, but how can that be? We only just met. He doesn't know me, and I don't know him. Our eyes stay locked until he turns back to the front of the line.

My gaze is lingering on his backside while he stands in line for our coffee and I wait at a little table in the corner. His waist is slim and shoulders are slightly wider. Perfectly proportioned. Irresistibly put together. The beard and tattoos seem to call you to make a particular conclusion about who Lenox Malone really is, but you'd be wrong. He is more than meets the eye. I see it beyond the surface; I just can't put my finger on exactly what it is.

He swivels in my direction again and catches me staring at him. When our eyes meet again, my heart quickens and a flutter of anxiety moves through me.

Walking toward me, coffee in hand, Lenox never looks away.

As he takes the seat across from me, he places my drink in front of me. "You okay?" he inquires. "You look a bit nervous. I hope it's not me," he continues.

"Oh…oh, no. No. I'm alright," I stutter out, almost shyly.

"Good, because I've waited…" he trails off. "I mean, I'm glad because I wouldn't want to scare you off already."

Tilting my head, I watch his expression. For a minute, I thought he was going to say something else, but he didn't.

"No, I'm good," I smile. "Thank you for this. I really needed it," I say as I lift the cup of hot liquid to my mouth and blow on it.

"You're welcome. It's the least I could do after I almost bowled you over," he says in jest.

Laughing, I shake my head. "Oh, no. I think it was the other way around. In fact, I should have bought you the cup of coffee," I joke back.

"The girl should never pay on the first date," he declares.

My eyes dart up to his face, and his eyes lock on me once again. Chills run up my arms because this one look makes me feel like we are the only two people around. A gentleman. A girl should never pay...on the first date?

Finally, my mind clears. "Date?"

A cocky grin lights up his face. "Yes, one day you'll think back on this day and think to yourself, I remember when Lenox and I went on our first date. We talked and laughed after he knocked me over, first on the sidewalk and then with his charms."

A burst of laughter escapes my lips. "You're pretty sure of yourself, aren't you?"

He continues grinning with a charming look of confidence. "It's a prediction, and most of it's come true already."

"What?" I respond and fail completely at keeping a serious look on my face.

Leaning forward across the table, his face so close to mine I can almost feel his breath. "Yep. We're talking and laughing, all I need to do is get you to agree to another date."

He sits back, crosses his arms. I noticed his biceps bulge and the tattoos stretching beautifully on his skin. When I look back up into his steely blue eyes, they're sparking. His lips are turned up into a confident grin.

"See? You already want to say yes, and I haven't even formally asked you," he declares.

Shaking my head, I deny his observation. "No."

"Say yes, Tessa. I know I'm getting ahead of myself, but I think you should give me a chance," he begs.

I hesitate, and he never takes his eyes off of me. There it is again, that familiarity between us. Thirty minutes ago, this guy was a virtual stranger, and now…now, it seems as if we've known one another for longer. Chad's voice whispers in my mind, *Do it.* My God, I hate when his voice pops into my head.

Reaching into my purse, I pull out a pen and sticky note. For a brief moment, my heart clenches at the thought of handwritten letters and journals professing love. *It doesn't matter,* I think to myself, quietly jotting down my number then pushing it across the table.

Before I can move my hand away, his covers mine. There it is again. A feeling that something is pulling me at my center just from the mere touch of his hand.

"I've got to go," I announce, yanking my hand back. Standing, I gather my things. "Thank you for the coffee."

He stands. "You're welcome. It's the least I could do."

Backing away, I give him a smile.

"I'll call you," he tells me. "I'm so glad we ran into one another."

The way he says it makes it seem as if he's been waiting for us to meet.

"So am, I," I say truthfully.

Turning hastily, I make my way out of the coffee shop feeling a strange sense of longing and overwhelming need to escape.

I have no idea how I'm going to be able to concentrate on this meeting, let alone another blind date.

***

Cute. Nice. Polite. I'm barely listening as my date, Jack animatedly recounts his hike last summer through the Grand Canyon. Damn it. I'm hardly listening. This is ridiculous.

Finally, Chad gets it right. He doesn't send me out with the Antichrist, and my mind is elsewhere. What's worse is that it isn't just somewhere else, it's on someone else.

Lenox Malone, to be exact. The handsome, rugged, semistranger that I spent all of thirty minutes with over coffee. Isn't that just my luck?

I've got to stop. He probably isn't that great anyway.

Oh, who am I kidding? I know that's a lie. He is probably every bit as incredible as I imagined him to be for the last three hours since I walked away from him at Java Joe's.

"Tessa…Tessa?"

Oh, shit. Jack is staring at me, repeating my name with a concerned look on his face.

"Boring you, huh?" he says with a perfect grin on his face.

"No!" I shout a little too loudly. Lowering my voice, I continue, "No, it's me. It's been a long day. I apologize for being so rude."

He laughs. "Don't worry about it. Should we order dessert?"

Looking at him, I can't find a single thing wrong. Get a grip, Tessa. Lenox could be awful. He may not even call. Jack is right in front of you.

"Yes, I would never pass up dessert," I reply.

I place a happy look on my face to reassure him, but I can feel my emotions preparing for battle internally. Damn, my luck.

May 12, 2011

Five years. For five years, I've loved Sara. I'll continue to love her. It's the easiest thing I've ever done.

CHAPTER 15

Lenox

"**Y**OU TOLD HER, DIDN'T YOU?" Sammy assumes, taking me a little off guard. All I did was walk in the room.

Pushing past him, I roll my eyes. I want to ignore him, but I know he'll only keep nagging at me.

"I took her to coffee," I answer, swiping my card to clock in.

When I turn around Sammy has a big goofy grin on his face. He looks like he just won the lottery.

"I hate to say I told you so, but well you know I'm not opposed to being right so," he pauses, waggling his eyes brows. "I told ya so."

I don't respond, but instead, keep my gaze fixed on Sammy. Debating if I should break it to him that although I went to coffee with Tessa, I didn't tell her I've been writing her letters for the last month. He'll want to know why I didn't tell her. I can't answer that question. I started to tell her several times. It crossed my mind multiple times as I watched her sitting at the table alone from a distance and when I looked into her eyes. I could see they were searching mine for something she couldn't quite pinpoint herself. I could see a reluctance and I chickened out. I couldn't bring myself to take the chance of missing an opportunity of getting to know her. Of her getting to know me.

"So, tell me. What did she say?" he asks. "Better yet, what did you say?"

Shaking my head, I laugh. "You're such a fucking girl sometimes." Pausing, I busy myself avoiding the conversation as long as possible when really it's inevitable. "I took her to coffee. I told her my name; she told me hers. It was nice." I turn to face him with my hands on my hips. "I didn't tell her I'm the one who's been writing her letters."

Freezing just before he swipes his card, he turns and looks at me.

"What the fuck?" This time, he shakes his head at me. "Lenox, you had the perfect opportunity, and you don't say anything. What's stopping you?"

"It didn't feel like the right time. What would I have said, exactly?" I swallow a deep breath. "She would have thought I was crazy."

"You think it's going to be better next time? I mean, you do plan on seeing her again, right?" He rolls his eyes. "Don't answer that because I know you do. I just don't know what is stopping you from telling her. Dude, it's not good you are keeping this from her. Girls hate lies, even small ones of non-admission."

"You think I don't fucking know this, man?"

"Honestly, Nox, I don't know what you're thinking anymore, but you're gonna do what you're gonna do. You just better figure out exactly what that is and soon or I'm afraid it won't turn out the way you want."

Walking away, Sammy leaves me wondering just exactly what it is I do want. The letter I wrote earlier, burning in a hypothetical hole in my pocket.

I pull into the driveway, shut the car off, and rest my forehead on the steering wheel. I spent the rest of the day thinking about Tessa and what I expect from all of this hanging between us.

Here is what I do know. I like the way she presents herself. Her laugh. Her smile. The feisty way she defends herself when she feels like she's being attacked or when she believes in something strongly. The scent of lilac that hangs in the air around her. It's so familiar and comforting, yet I can't recall ever knowing the smell before.

Releasing a long sigh, I get out of the car and head to the house.

It's quiet when I walk through the door except for the soft purring coming from Roosevelt as he brushes against my legs in greeting. I reach down and pick him up in the attempt of giving him some attention, but he quickly wiggles himself from my arms. Damn, cat.

Walking over to the couch, I fall back on it, putting my head back and closing my eyes.

I've got to figure this out. Sammy's right as much as I hate to admit it. I need to be upfront with Tessa about who I am and my connection to the letters. I'll just write her a few more letters and see her before I tell her. This way she will know me and know I'm not crazy. She'll know me, and I'll still be able to show her that romance lives.

Even as I think this is the best way to handle this situation, an unsure feeling nags me, but I push it away.

Pulling the letter from my pocket, I tear it in half and start over.

It's been nearly a week since I literally ran into Tessa and took her to coffee. I've mulled over what I want to do and how to handle this almost every minute. I've come up with very little and decided it will just come to me when it's the right time.

As "letter guy," I can't contact her until Thursday when I can leave the letter for her, but as Lenox, nothing is stopping me.

Pulling out the pink sticky note, my heartbeat stutters briefly as my eyes roam over her handwriting and phone number. It's almost funny to think that a pink sticky note sort of started this all. God, it annoyed the shit out of me at first. The pure fact that she wrote that first message on one and just stuck it on my door. It was…it was just so fucking cute, and I hated it.

Now I would take a thousand pink sticky notes if it meant I could talk to her every day.

Picking up my phone, I tap out her phone number.

Lenox: *Hello, this is Lenox Malone. We met the other day and had coffee. I'm sure you're surprised to hear from me since it's been almost a week. I've thought about you.*

I sound like an idiot, but I keep going.

Lenox: *I was wondering if you might be interested in going to lunch tomorrow?*

I put my phone on the table and walk away. She may not answer right away. I won't even think about it. Oh, who am I kidding? It's all I'll reflect on until she texts back. My text tone chimes through the room, causing my heart rate to speed up.

Tessa: *Really? Did you just ask me out through a text message? Shame on you, Lenox Malone. I pegged you for a more romantic sort of guy.*

I laugh then realize maybe she isn't trying to be funny.

Lenox: *I did. Was that a mistake?*
Tessa: *I don't know, was it?*

Okay, now she's cute. This is the girl I remember exchanging emails with a couple of months ago. The one that can dish out a plate full of snark, yet remain utterly charming.

Lenox: *It's only a mistake if your answer is no.*

Tessa: *Ha. Well, I'm not sure I should accept a date with a guy I barely know who can't even find it in him to pick up the phone and call me to ask me.*

This girl. She's going to be the end of me. She seems so confident now. If she wants a phone call, then a phone call is exactly what she's going to get.

October 5, 2011

The air around us is changing. My class schedule has been tough this semester. I've been studying hard, and it's been my primary focus. My grades dropped, and I can't let that happen. It's part of my scholarship. I work, and I make the grades. Sara told me she was feeling my absence. I told her it won't be much longer and to hold on to the fact she knows I love her. I do. I do love you, Sara.

CHAPTER 16

TESSA

HOLDING MY PHONE IN MY hand, I wait for his response. I'd be lying if I said I wasn't having a little fun at his expense. While the text thing is a bit of a cop-out these days, it really doesn't bother me all that much. Honestly, I was just excited that he contacted me at all. I was beginning to wonder if he ever would or if our one coffee encounter was all for the show.

Suddenly, the ring of my phone echoes through my office, startling me.

Staring down at the flashing screen my cheeks heat when I realize it's him. Oh shit. It's him. Although I teased him the only way I would say yes to lunch would be if he called, I didn't really expect him to do it. Suck it up, Tessa. You've got this.

I swipe my finger across the screen, accepting the call.

"Hi," I answer timidly.

What the hell is wrong with my voice. Oh God.

I hear him laugh through the phone. "You sound a little surprised which is weird since you're the one who insisted I was an asshole for not calling you to ask you to lunch."

"I did not call you an asshole," I defend myself.

"Fine, in not so many words, but you most definitely insinuated it." The phone quiets for a moment before he continues. "So this is me calling. I want to see you again, Tessa. Have lunch with me tomorrow. Please?"

Taken off guard by the muted desperation in his voice, I freeze.

He was great the other day. Charming and funny not to mention incredibly good looking. Why not? I can't think of one reason.

"Tessa?" I hear his voice rasp through the phone when I don't answer.

"Yes," I whisper.

"Yes?" he repeats like a question like he isn't sure he understood me right.

"Yes, Lenox Malone. I'll have lunch with you tomorrow." My face lights up in anticipation.

"See?" he asks me, and I have no idea what he's talking about.

"See, what?" I inquire back.

"A second date means we are another date closer to the day you recall what made you fall in love with me. Remember my prediction," he states with that same confidence he had the other day, and I can imagine the crooked grin on his face.

"Don't you think you're getting a little ahead of yourself?" I retort because I refuse to play along with his ridiculous prediction.

"We'll see, Tessa. We'll see. I'll meet you tomorrow at eleven forty-five in front of your building. Bye, beautiful."

He hangs up before I even have a chance to respond. He's insane. And possibly the most charming guy I've met.

The day flew by and my mind raced along with it, thoughts of Lenox Malone consuming my thoughts. That is until Chad walked into my office.

"You've been daydreaming all day. Journal boy, again?" Chad asks, a smirk on his face as he props himself with one hip on my desk.

My cheeks color and my stomach churns. The conflicting feelings I'm having are new to me. This would only happen to me. Two guys when only a couple of weeks ago, I couldn't meet a single man worth my time. Who knows, maybe these twos aren't worth my time either. Something is telling me I'm wrong.

Chad is still staring at me with a knowing grin on his face. Except he doesn't know. I never told him about Lenox because he would've made a bigger deal out of it than it needs to be.

"Actually, no." The smile leaves his face. "It's someone else. I met him last week. We had coffee," I continue. His right eyebrow shoots up. "He was nice."

Adjusting himself on my desk, Chad watches me a moment.

"You're only telling me about him now? I'm hurt," he says in mock betrayal, placing his hand over his heart.

Rolling my eyes, I lean forward in my chair and place my chin in my hands.

"There isn't much to tell. He's handsome and seems kind." I smile at the memory of Lenox sitting across from me, a gleam in his eyes, and the familiar way his eyes caressed my face. "He's also confident and flirty."

"Handsome, kind, confident, and flirty—this sounds promising. So, what's special about today if you met him last week?" Chad asks, wanting more.

My cheeks color again. My god, what is wrong with me.

"He called me today and asked me to lunch tomorrow." I release a loud sigh. "Chad, I've gone on, at least, ten dates in the last month. All but one was a total disaster. He was great, but I couldn't get those letters or that journal out of my mind. Then I meet Lenox."

Chad interrupts me. "His name is Lenox? The name alone is a panty dropper."

Laughing, I slap him on his arm with the back of my hand.

"Be serious," I say.

Grinning, he says, "I am."

Shaking my head, I continue, "Well, I guess it's true." I laugh.

"I don't know what is going on. There was something about him. Something so familiar, but I can't get the guy from the letters off my mind either."

"Babydoll, I think you need to go with the flow and see what happens. You don't need to control everything."

Chad stands up, walks over, and places a kiss on the top of my head. I watch him as he walks out of my office.

He's right. I just need to go with the flow and see what happens. If I worry too much about what will happen then, I might miss something. I may not know what I'm feeling, but I do know I'm not willing to miss out.

Coffee in hand, I rush into my office, throwing my purse onto my desk. From the corner of my eye, I catch a glimpse of an envelope falling to the floor. An envelope with my name on it. My heart races with anticipation as I pick it up.

How does he keep doing this? I may not know what to think about this situation, but I know the way it makes me feel. Hopeful. Happy. Wanted.

As I slowly bend down to pick up the envelope, my heart begins racing.

Why does this make me so nervous? Is nervous even the right word for it? Especially when I feel good knowing he has written to me. Written words specifically for me. Maybe Chad is right; I can't stand being out of control with of my emotions. I'm so used to the idea of being disappointed by guys and not expecting anything from them. It leaves me in control. I've always been able to keep my feet on solid ground in any relationship I've ever been in until now. In just a few months, I have not one, but two guys making my world unsteady.

Sitting down at my desk, I stare at the envelope, allowing my fingertips to rub over my name. It's almost as if I can see him, this mystery guy whispering my name, over and over again. Calling to some emotion, buried deep inside, waiting to be claimed.

I take a deep breath in as I open the envelope and pull the letter from inside. As I unfold it, my hands shake just as they have done every letter before this one.

Releasing the breath, I begin reading.

Tessa,

I'm sure you started to think I may never reply to you. I'm sorry it took me some time. If I'm honest, this isn't my original letter. I wrote a different one, but it isn't the time. I'll explain another time, but I do want to address your reply to me.

I always find it fascinating when people love the color yellow. It seems to be the one color that never gets the credit it deserves. People always immediately think of school buses, but is that really yellow? Yellow has given us so much more beauty than acknowledged. Sunflowers and the pretty middle splash of color in a daisy. It's the color of sunshine and summer days. The color of a refreshing glass of lemonade. And butter! Butter makes everything better! (sorry, I'm getting a little excited)

A burst of laughter explodes from me; my cheeks are starting to hurt. I can't stop smiling. Who is this guy? He's so strange, but I like it. I like him and the way his words make me feel. When I gain some composure, I pick up where I left off.

You just made me realize how great the color yellow is if I think about it. I'm thinking about it, Tessa. I'm thinking about you. I think you just might be that great, too.

Speaking of great: Will Johnson? You surprised me, and I'm never surprised. Not only did you surprise me, but you impressed me. He's pretty awesome and one of my all-time favorites. Call Call Call is a unique choice of favorite songs.

I want you to keep surprising me. Keep impressing me. It's your turn. Ask me questions because the point of all of this is for us to get to know one another. Share ourselves. Be real. Be honest. See where it all takes us and one day...

Who knows? The only thing I know is I want to know more. I'll share with you things I wouldn't typically share, and I hope you'll do the same. That is romance.

Romance is what we're searching for, right?

Give me romance, Tessa. Tell me more.

Xoxo, Me

Falling. Although I'm sitting down, I feel like I'm falling. How is it these simple words make me want to tell him more. Want to know him more. Just want.

Shit, I'm in deep trouble. Maybe deep confusion is a better way to put it. Between this letter and lunch, I'm not going to be able to concentrate on a single damn thing today.

April 10, 2012

As I approach my 23rd birthday, I think about all I've done. All I've accomplished. All I have left to do. For being so young, I've always known what I want for my life. I want to help people, and I want to love.

CHAPTER 17

Lenox

WALKING UP TO THE FRONT of her building, I realize I'm more nervous than I thought. Surely she found my letter, and now we're having lunch. Except, Tessa doesn't know the letter is from me. She doesn't know she's having lunch with the guy who wrote the letter.

Now I want to know what she does think.

She said she wanted to see where this takes us. She accepted my challenge, but that was before she met Lenox.

What the fuck am I saying? I'm Lenox. Huffing out a breath, I want to punch myself for being so fucking stupid. How is this going to work?

Just as I consider walking away, Tessa walks through the doors. Her face lights up with a timid smile when she sees me standing there waiting for her. My face mirrors hers, my chest tingles at the sight of her. Too late, Malone. You're a goner.

My mind wanders for a moment, thinking about if she found the letter. What did she think? Once again I remember, to Tessa, I didn't write the letter.

I take a few steps toward her, and when we're toe to toe, I smile wider. "Hi," I say. Shit, who's voice is that? I didn't sound like myself. It was almost raspy.

She looks down at her feet and then back up until our eyes meet.

"Uh, hi," she says nervously. Pushing a stray piece of hair behind her ear. "It's good to see you," she continues.

Gazing into her eyes, I swallow a hard lump in my throat. She is so beautiful. There is something in her eyes, a part of her I think most people would miss, a beautiful piece, and I'm so thankful I'm not missing it. I want this to work. I want all of this to work because I want to see all of her. All of the parts she hides beneath the blue hue of her eyes.

"Shall we?" I take her hand and loop it around my arm and look at her expectantly.

Her eyes become brighter, and she nods as if she were at a loss for words.

For the first few minutes we don't speak, walking side by side in companionable silence.

Suddenly, she breaks the quiet between us. "Where are you taking me?"

Without looking at her, I reply, "I thought we would walk over to the Iron Cactus. They have great lunch specials during the week. Is that okay?"

"Of course, it's one of my favorite places to have lunch."

Her response sends an unreasonable amount of happiness through me. It feels great knowing I pleased her. Damn it; I'm not just a goner. I'm gone.

Sitting across from her at a table on the rooftop patio, I notice the way the sun highlights her hair. It leaves a sort of halo effect on her. She seems as nervous as I am with the way she keeps looking at me from the tops of her eyes as she scans the menu. She's caught me more than once watching her. I should be embarrassed, but I'm not. I can't help watching her.

Damn it; she catches me again and this time, she doesn't look back down. Without taking her eyes from mine, she closes the menu.

"Did you decide?" I ask to deter her from asking why I've been ogling her.

I can see it in her eyes; she's curious, yet she isn't sure she should ask. I recognize the moment she decides to be brave. I like it. I like it so much I almost don't care I'm going to have to tell her that I can't keep my eyes off of her because she's the most incredible woman I've laid my eyes on.

Her eyebrow shoots up, letting me know she isn't going to let it pass.

"Yes, did you?" I want to laugh because I can see the battle going on in her mind just by looking at her face. "Why do you keep looking at me like that?"

I keep my face neutral.

"Like what?" Again, it takes everything I have to hold back.

Before she can say anything, the waitress arrives and takes our order. Our eyes never leave the other as we give our order to her. Who knows what is going through her mind as she writes it all down, but she walks away after saying she will have our food right out.

"So?" It comes out like a question. Tessa apparently isn't letting it go.

I can't help the happy expression I give her. "I don't know how to answer that question." Pausing, I try to find the right words, so I don't scare her away. "Let's just say I like you. Not only because I like looking at you, but it's something in your eyes. It makes me want to discover everything I can about you."

Running a hand through my hair, I break eye contact with her. Her gaze became so intense; I had to look away. I peer back at her, and she's smiling. I lift my head a little higher and return the expression.

She breaks the silence first. "Well, ask me something...anything." Her voice comes out a little breathy; I can tell she surprised herself by the look that just crossed her features.

Good. She's feeling it, too. This pull between us. It overwhelms me. Scares me. I've felt this before, but it's more intense with Tessa. I want to know why, but I don't. I'm playing a dangerous game with her. Leaving this Lenox and the letter Lenox separate is safe. I need safe until I can be sure.

"I'd like to be friends. Let's start there. Tell me about you and your work," I propose.

Is that a look of relief I just saw? She does feel it, too.

Blushing, Tessa nods her head. "I think we're going to be friends, Lenox Malone." Tapping her finger on her chin playfully, she pretends to be thinking. "I guess I'll start from the beginning," she suggests. The playful tone still present in her voice. She's enjoying this as much as I am.

I hang on every word as she tells me about herself. We joke and the conversation flows between us.

Yes, we're definitely going to be friends.

I floated on cloud nine the rest of the day. Not even Sammy's comments about me being a pansy could deter my mood.

As I drive down my street, Tessa is on my mind. All the little facts I learned about her. The way she bites her lips when she's embarrassed. Even the way she rolls her eyes when she thinks I'm ridiculous. All of it is so natural. So familiar. Yet, we were both still holding back. I realized it when she paused between sentences. Or when she changed the subject if things were too personal.

I can't blame her. I did the same thing. Held back even though everything in me screamed to give into what felt right. She felt right.

When I'm just a few houses down from my driveway, I see her. Pushing my brakes, I come to almost a complete stop. Taken off guard by her presence. Pulling to the side of the street, so she doesn't notice me, I watch her.

Tessa darts across the road and onto my porch.

My heart beats rapidly at the sight of her. It would be so simple to continue to drive home, revealing myself to her. So easy yet so hard. I don't move and just watch her. She isn't there long.

I know why she's here and irrationally, I'm filled with jealousy. I'm jealous of myself because she is leaving a note for the guy who wrote her a letter. She had lunch with me today, and now she's leaving a note for someone else. Okay, not someone else. Me. But, she doesn't know that we are the same person. Shit, this is a fucking mess.

She dashes back to her car, glancing back once before getting in her car and pulling away.

As soon as her taillights disappear down the road, I pull back on the street, continuing home. I feel discomfort in the pit of my stomach. Turning off the car, I sit for a moment, my head against the steering wheel. Thinking of Tessa and our lunch date. Going over the things I know about her. Wondering how she might react to our situation if she knew everything.

Opening the door, I get out and make my way to the front door where I know her response to my last letter waits.

When I reach the door, just as I suspect, the pink sticky note is there, except this time there are multiple pink-colored notes. Not just one this time, but three. I pull each one off, unlock the door and drop my things as soon as I walk through the threshold. The pieces of square papers still firmly gripped in my hand.

Taking a seat on the couch, I begin reading.

You're funny. I like it. Yes, yellow doesn't get enough credit. Neither does Will Johnson, well at least in the mainstream music world. Maybe he likes it that way. I would. I'm also impressed by your knowledge of his music. Can I say that I didn't think this whole sticky note through? I thought it fit to use them since our beginning was on a sticky note, but it makes it

DIFFICULT TO GIVE YOU TOO MUCH ON
JUST ONE.
I WANT TO ASK YOU SO MANY THINGS.
DO I WANT TO KNOW WHY?
WHY ARE YOU DOING THIS?
WHAT IS LOVE TO YOU?
YOU SAID YOU NO LONGER BELIEVE
IN ROMANCE...IN LOVE.
WHAT MADE YOU STOP?

TELL ME YOUR FAVORITE COLOR.

TELL ME WHAT MAKES YOU SMILE.

TELL ME WHAT MAKES
YOUR HEART RACE.

When I finish reading, my head falls against the back of the couch. This girl has me all tangled up, and I'm worried it's already too late. Too late to be cautious. Too late to go slow.

December 30, 2012

A couple of days and we'll be ringing in the new year. Sara and I have agreed 2013 will be our year to focus on us again. My schedule is a little lighter, and hers is too. We keep holding on just like I knew we would. Every day we hold on is another day closer to what we're destined for in this life.

CHAPTER 18

TESSA

I 'M A TRAMP. OKAY, THAT'S a little harsh. Lots of girls go out with lots of guys. It's called dating. I glance up from my drink, across the table at my latest blind date. Damn Chad. This is it. This is the last one.

The guy seems nice enough. Not as nice as Jack, but more pleasant than any of the other guys. Definitely not as nice as Lenox. Or even "letter boy," as Chad and I have taken to calling him.

Charlie isn't being rude to the waiter, or me, or yelling on his phone, or feeling me up under the table. It's good, but it's all messed up. He's talking, but I'm not listening. The guilt started to get to me about twenty minutes ago. Twenty minutes ago, I ordered a Mexican Martini with extra jalapeno olives…extra dirty. Dirty. Just thinking about being extra dirty makes me giggle.

It also makes the guilt I'm feeling worse because I'm thinking of being dirty with another guy. No, two other guys. Wait. Just to be clear, not two guys together, but separate. One doesn't even have a face, and one has everything. I giggle again. That's when I hear my date; his voice pulls me out of my alcohol induced daydream.

"Umm, are you okay?" he looks a bit mortified.

I stare at him thinking about how to answer that question.

Well, Charlie, I think. *Not really. I'm on a date with a nice enough guy. But, Charlie, the problem is I can't stop thinking about these other two guys. And I'm tipsy. A little tipsy and if I keep drinking these delicious concoctions full of tequila then I will be even less okay.* Shit. He's still waiting for my answer. Charlie thinks I'm nuts. I just saw the look flash in his eyes.

"I'm sorry," I blurt out. "You're great. This place is great." I raise my arms in the air and open them palms up like I'm Vanna White presenting a prize on the Wheel of Fortune. I am nuts. Oh, shit. I'm the "bad" date this time. I think I might cry. "Oh, God. I'm sorry."

Charlie smiles at me sympathetically. "It's fine, Tessa. I get it. Maybe we should call it a night," he suggests.

"I'm sorry. Are you sure? It's not..."

He puts his hand up as he stands. "Please don't say it," he pleads with a grin.

Fudge nugget. I was about to say it's not him, it's me. Dear lord, I hate myself right now. No, I hate Chad. This is his fault. And the letter boys. And Lenox Malone's fault.

"Okay, I won't," I try to grin back.

"I'll take you home," he offers. He reaches his hand out to me.

Shaking my head, I politely decline his offer. "It's fine. I think I will finish my drink and call an Uber." I stand up and give him a friendly hug. "Thank you for a lovely evening."

We both give one another one last smile before he walks away, and I sit back down in front of my drink.

Shit, now what. Pulling out my phone, I hit the speed dial.

"Where are you?" I wait for an answer. "Oh yeah, it was just great. So fantastic that he just left, and I'm sitting here at the restaurant drinking alone."

Chad's laugh echoes through the phone. I hold it away from my ear.

"I hope you know I hate you." I listen to him as he continues to laugh at me. "It's not funny."

I look around the restaurant because I swear everyone in here is staring at me, the pathetic girl sipping her martini all alone.

"Fine, I'll be there in fifteen minutes, and you better be prepared to grovel at my high-heeled feet."

Hanging up, so I don't have to listen to his cackle over the phone any longer, I throw a little extra tip on the table and head out the door. He says he'll cheer me up. He better because I need reassurance that I haven't lost my mind.

When I walk into the club, I head straight for the bar. Chad said he was with a group of friends. I make my way through the crowd and quickly push my way to the front. Once I order, I turn, leaning my back against the bar, scanning the room for Chad.

He must have already spotted me because he is walking straight for me.

"What's up, buttercup?" he asks cheerfully. I can tell he thinks he can sweeten me up with his terms of endearments.

"Just stop right there, mister. We are going to get one thing straight right now," I insist.

He looks at me, his eyes twinkling with mischief, and winks. I groan and fold my arms across my chest. Chad takes me by the arms and pulls me into a hug.

"What is it?" he asks seriously as he strokes a hand over my back. "You know I'll do anything for you, so what is it?"

"I don't want to go on any more dates. I want you to stop setting me up," I mumble into his chest.

Chad turns me around, takes my drink from the bartender then hands it to me. Bending at the knees a little, so we are eye to eye, he sighs. "Fine. I just want you to be happy. I want you to know that there are good guys out there even if you have to sort through the bad ones first. I mean, how else can you recognize the good ones?"

Damn it; I hate when he makes so much sense. It's so annoying.

Chad leads me through the crowd to a table with a couple of barstools. His friends are nowhere in sight, most likely huddled up in the corner, throwing back shots.

We both take a seat; he leans in close so I can hear him over the loud music and chatter.

"Okay, out with it, what happened?" Chad demands gently. This is so typical of our relationship. He pushes me to live my life until he thinks I might break. It may seem selfish, but I know he loves me. Chad is the one person I know I can count on to give me honesty, no matter what. He is the one person I can completely rely on.

"I happened," I moan. It may sound like a vague statement, but Chad gets me. I know because his eyebrows immediately shoot up when the words leave my mouth. "Romantic letters happened. Lenox Malone happened."

I toast the air with my drink before downing it.

Laughing, Chad takes the glass from me. "Whoa, girl. Slow down."

"They're breaking me down. In a short time, they've both started chipping away at the carefully constructed walls I've put up around my heart for years," I whine. Lifting my hand to signal the cocktail waitress so I can order another drink, I continue, "It scares the shit out of me. Let's face it, these feelings they're stirring in me can't end well. End being the key word, Chad. We both know it always ends."

The look of disappointment and pity in his eyes makes me cringe. He has always hated the fact I just can't trust things will work out some day. One of the things I've always admired about Chad is his eternal optimism and belief in people. He never lets a little heartache deter him from searching for that one person who might change his world. I should believe love exists. My parents are the perfect example of lasting, genuine romantic love. It's ridiculous, but I think it may be the main reason I have a hard time taking a chance. What if I can't live up to their love story?

"Honey, you've got to stop overthinking things. It isn't good for you," he stresses. "You act like you need to choose one or the other right now. You don't. Consider yourself lucky because you have options. You aren't hurting anyone. You aren't committed."

"God, I wish I had your confidence. I wish I could move through life believing things will just work out the way they are supposed to work out," I admit.

The waitress walks up, interrupting us. "What'll it be?"

"Another Mexican martini, extra dirty, please," I tell her then look at Chad. He shakes his head and turns to me as the girl in the mini skirt walks away.

"Tessa Collins, you need to stop this ridiculousness. Let it be. Enjoy being admired by multiple men and I'll refrain from anymore set ups. The rest will fall into place. See what happens without all of the pressure," he scolds. "Now let's have some fun."

As those words leave Chad's mouth, the waitress walks back up with my drink. I thank her, take a sip and pick the toothpick up, pulling the jalapeno stuffed olive off with my teeth. All the while my eyes roam over the crowd surrounding us.

"Let's dance," Chad shouts.

"Damn, I love these..." I begin to say before my eyes lock on a single face in the crowd. "Oh, holy fuck!" I nearly choke on the olive.

June 23, 2013

College graduation came and went. Now do I go to grad school or not. Sara says she'll support me no matter what I decide, but something is off. I'm not sure what it is, and dread overcomes me. Sara says she loves me. I know I love her. Everything will work out

CHAPTER 19

Lenox

I WATCH AS THE GIRL Sammy is with clings to his side like she would fall over if he wasn't there. Her friend, which Sammy apparently failed to mention when he invited me out tonight is laughing at something he just said. Her laugh is a high pitched shriek I'm sure is caused by the large amount of alcohol she's consumed over the last hour.

Speaking of drinking, I look down at my beer and realize it's empty.

Standing, I tell them I'm going to get a refill. They're so engrossed in their conversation they don't pay any attention to the fact I didn't wait for a response.

As I make my way to the bar, I look around at the crowd around me. I take in my surroundings, watching girls dance with guys, groups of friends laughing and taking shots, everyone enjoying the night. I look back at the table I just left thinking about Sammy's lame attempt to get me out of the house and dating again. I'm not interested. Well, I'm not interested in just anyone. I'm interested in only one person.

Turning my attention back to the bar, I push through a small crowd, looking through the hordes of people; I stop dead in my tracks. What are the odds? There she is, in the same bar as me, sitting with another guy. I regard them, taking in the way he leans in closer to her and her response is one of familiarity. There's an intimacy to it, but it doesn't appear romantic. I blow out a breath that I didn't know I was holding.

My lips curl at the corners as I watch her take a sip of her drink then pull the olive into her mouth with her teeth. Like a magnet, our gazes snap together. I nearly bust out laughing at the look on her face and the words I read on her lips. She's just as surprised to see me as I am to see her. I can't tell if she is happy or disappointed, but I guess we'll find out. It's not like I can just ignore the fact she has seen me.

Moving toward her as if a rope pulls me, my eyes never leave hers.

I barely catch the fact her friend is now staring at me, too. A crooked smile is lighting his face, highlighting his attractiveness even more. Man, I hope he's a friend.

"Tessa Collins." Her name leaves my lips in a rush once I reach her. I don't even recognize my voice. Her cheeks are a rosy pink color and her eyes slightly glossy. She's beautiful. My stomach does a flip making me feel off balance. I put my hand on the table in front of me to steady myself.

Gaping at me through a hazy gaze, Tessa doesn't move. Neither do I. Suddenly, the guy next to her elbows her in the side.

Snapping out of it, Tessa stands abruptly. Straightening her skirt and top, she pushes her shoulders back. I want to laugh because she looks a little tipsy which explains her dazed stare.

"Well, Lenox Malone. What…what are the odds?" she stutters out.

"My thoughts exactly. I guess it's my lucky night." I beam. I can't help myself. This girl makes everything in me come alive.

Once again our eyes are locked, and the world around us disappears. Well, that's until her companion makes himself known by shoving his hand in my face.

"Soooooo, you're Lenox," he says in an exaggerated tone. His eyes are roaming over me from head to toe approvingly.

Looking from his hand to his face and back again, I finally take it in mine and shake it.

"Uh, yes," I say, confused. He knows me.

His smile widens and begins to rattle on. "My girl has told me so much about you, but in true Tessa fashion, she muted all of your best qualities." His eyes never leave me.

"Uh." I'm at a loss for words. I glance over at Tessa, and she's looking back and forth between this other guy and me.

"How rude of me. I'm Chad, Tessa's best friend, and gatekeeper," he jokes. I think.

His words snap Tessa out of her daydream; she slaps him on the arm.

"God, Chad," she says, obviously embarrassed because her cheeks turn a deeper shade of red. Turning her attention back to me, she gives me an awkward smile. "Lenox, this is my best friend until one minute ago, Chad."

"You love me." Chad scoffs before turning back to me. "It really is a pleasure. Now, Tess, I'm off to find Kari and Thomas," he says as he kisses her on each cheek. He lingers a moment next to her ear when he pulls her into a hug. "Lenox Malone is here in the tasty flesh, not in a letter. Stake a claim." As he pushes away, Tessa's eyes lock on mine. "Tah-tah, buttercup!"

Is it possible for your heart to soar and break at the same time? I think mine just did. *Get a hold of yourself, Lenox. He's talking about you either way. They just don't know it.*

We watch as Chad flits his way through the crowd to find what I'm assuming are his other friends. Leaving us, alone. My eyes drift back to Tessa; she still has her gaze locked on Chad, almost like she is afraid for him to leave. Do I scare her?

Slowly, her head turns to me, her eyes drifting up until they meet mine.

We don't move. We don't speak. For longer than socially acceptable, we just stand in front of one another. Watching. Waiting for the other to make a move.

I couldn't tell you how much time goes by before one of us moves. It's like we're both experiencing something within us we aren't sure how to handle. We aren't sure where to begin.

Although, we've been on one, no make that two dates, being in her presence throws me off. Maybe it's my small omission of the truth. The truth that I knew Tessa in some form before I ran into her that day outside of her building. Maybe it's the fact now that I've spent some time with her I'm drawn to her even more.

She speaks first. "Do you want to sit down?"

"Sure," I answer quickly, not even giving Sammy and his friends a second thought. "Can I buy you a drink?"

We take a seat across from one another as I catch the attention of the waitress who signals she will be with us in a moment.

She swallows hard, glancing at her practically full drink in front of her, then back to me. "Why not?" she responds, looking like she's questioning her judgment on the decision then she picks up the martini glass in front of her and throws it back. Drinking the remaining alcohol in one swallow, she blinks back the tears that pool in the corner of her eyes. My lip quirks up in one corner. She's nervous. Good, so am I.

When the cocktail waitress arrives to take our order, I quickly spout out my order at her. "I'll have a Sierra Nevada," I say then look to Tessa. "Tessa?"

She's watching the waitress with a curious look then lifts her glass. "I'll have another, extra dirty."

My mind drifts to other thoughts as I watch her lips say "extra dirty." I need to stop. My gaze stays locked on Tessa. She isn't even paying attention to me. Tessa is solely focused on the waitress.

I take the opportunity to study her. To study every curve of her face. Her beauty is so natural, so understated. In a way, she scares the shit out of me. The feelings she induces inside the deepest parts of me. This girl just might be my end, and I'm beginning to think the risk might be worth it.

December 4, 2013

I decided on grad school, but I've taken a semester off. I've been volunteering at the local Boys and Girls Club while working at the record store. Sammy is working there, too. Sara has taken some time off, and we're hoping she gets the job at the big marketing firm downtown. We're keeping things together. I'll be moving into the house my grandparents left me soon. I still have that uneasy feeling about things changing, but so far everything has stayed the same.

CHAPTER 20

TESSA

IS THIS HAPPENING? LENOX IS sitting across from me, signaling the waitress. I'm still feeling the shock from the surprise of running into him here. Especially when Chad and I were discussing Lenox and my situation involving him.

He's so damn attractive. The way his hair sticks up in every direction like he just rolled out of bed. The scruff of a beard, giving him a mysterious vibe that makes you want to uncover all of his secrets. The tattoos are accenting every muscle in his arms. Holy hell, he makes my insides melt.

When the waitress reaches our table, he smiles. It's a natural smile, but the dark haired girl with the beautiful alabaster skin blushes. It only accentuates her attractiveness. Lenox is oblivious, and it surprises me.

He orders a Sierra Nevada and turns to me for my order.

The girl taking our order reluctantly turns to me. I order the same drink I had earlier. She nods at me, taking one last longing look at Lenox and walks away.

I watch her retreat in disappointment. I don't know why, but I feel sorry for her. I admire her confidence and her attempt to draw his attention to her. She is pretty. I guess I'm trying to figure out why he didn't notice. Unreasonably comparing her to myself because I can feel his gaze burning into me and I can't understand why.

When I finally turn my attention back to Lenox, his mouth is curled up, his eyes crinkled at the corners with amusement on his face.

"What?" I question him, a bit afraid of his answer.

"Nothing." He pauses like he's trying to find the right words. "I'm glad we ran into one another," he finally says.

Before I could think about what I was saying, I agreed. "Me too."

I know I only said two words, but I'm certain the look on my face said so much more.

We make small talk until our drinks arrive a few minutes later. Once again the petite server tries to gain Lenox's notice to no avail. Part of me wants to say, "aha! He's mine so give it up." But, he isn't mine. I'm not even sure what I feel about him other than pure attraction.

Lenox passes her the money for our drinks, and she walks away.

He takes a long pull from his beer, setting it down, linking his fingers together before resting his chin on them. Staring at me, Lenox suddenly gets a mischievous grin on his face. I can tell he is about to say something, so I wait, worrying my lip from nervousness.

"It looks like I might be psychic," he announced.

"What?" I look at him like he's crazy, but maybe I'm the crazy one. Lenox Malone's face is beginning to blur. Uh oh.

He takes another swig before speaking. "Well, the way I see it, this is our third date. We are well on our way to fulfilling my prophecy."

I can't do anything but laugh, and it isn't because he's funny. Although his confidence when it comes to me is a little funny because he has no idea how right he is. Nope, I'm not laughing about that at all. That's not funny. Actually, I have no idea why I'm laughing. I down the rest of my drink and pop the last olive in my mouth.

"This. Is. Not. A Date," I state slowly and clearly. Okay, maybe not so clearly, but I'm almost sure I said it slowly. Almost.

Shit. I've got to get out of here. I've got to go home.

"I've got to go home," I blurt out abruptly. I begin to stand up, only swaying a little. This is just great.

Lenox jumps up and rushes around the table.

"Tessa, you're not driving. I'll take you home," he informs me.

Giggling, I pat his cheek. "I'm not driving, silly; I'll call for a ride."

He puts his hand over mine. It feels nice. He gives my palm a gentle kiss.

"Tessa, I'm not letting you go alone. I'll make sure you get home safely. I insist," Lenox asserts as he begins to pull me by my hand, leading me through the crowd and out of the bar.

I can't be sure, but I think we pass a grinning Chad on the way out.

We're standing outside of the bar; Lenox has his arm wrapped around my waist holding me against him. I rest my head on his chest. I shouldn't be resting my head on his chest. I shouldn't have had that last drink. That's a lot of shouldn't haves in one night. It feels so good just to rest my head here, what will it hurt? I'm so tired.

"Tessa, I'm going to need you to stay awake so you can give the driver your address, okay?" Lenox tells me, his voice whispering in my ear. His arm tightens around me. "Tessa?"

Nodding my head, I murmur, "Okay."

"Good." He sounds relieved.

I'm not sure how long we wait, but suddenly Lenox is lifting me into the car. He closes the door, and I presume walks around to the other side because he's sliding in beside me and lifting my head, resting it in his lap.

"Tessa, I'm going to need you tell him your address now," he informs me, gently brushing my hair off my cheek.

I mumble my address and hear Lenox repeat it to the driver. The car begins moving, and I feel myself drifting off. In and out of consciousness, I only register the soft touch of Lenox's thumb against my skin.

"Lenox?" I whisper his name.

"Yeah," he responds almost instantly.

"I'm sorry, I don't usually drink like I did tonight," I apologize.

"Tessa, I'm not judging you," he tries to reassure me.

I reach up for his hand, pulling it down against my chest, holding it tightly. He doesn't stop me. A couple of minutes go by before either of us speaks.

"I'm just so confused, Lenox. So confused," I confess so quietly I'm not even sure he heard me.

He doesn't move, doesn't speak; he remains completely still. If he says anything to me, I never hear it before my eyes close.

July 29, 2014

I'm starting school again in a few weeks. Sara has been working a lot, so I've been spending more time volunteering. I've been acting like a big brother to one boy in particular, who seems to need guidance. I realize I could've been this kid if I hadn't been blessed with a mom like mine. Mom, tells me she is so happy

I'm living the life I've always wanted, but I question if that's true. I didn't imagine this is how my life with Sara would be. Nine years and I love her. I'm just not sure Sara is happy. I'm not sure how to make us happy again.

CHAPTER 21

Lenox

NUDGING TESSA AWAKE AND LIFTING her out of the car, I walk her up to her loft. Once she digs her keys out of her purse and opens the door, I guide her in the direction she indicated I could find her room.

I lead her to the bed, turning to leave as she falls back on it, unbuttoning her jeans.

"Don't go," she shouts, reaching one arm toward me awkwardly. "I need your help getting undressed."

A chill runs up my spine at the thought of undressing her. I should turn around and walk away. I should leave.

"Tessa," I say huskily. She has no idea what she's doing to me.

Suddenly, she stands up, pulling at her jeans, trying to take them off. She is wobbling on her feet, practically falling over, but puts her hand out just in time to catch herself on the bed. I want to laugh. I want to run away from this girl and every emotion she makes me feel.

Walking over to her, I grab her around the waist, steadying her on her feet. She looks up at me, lips curling up in an attractive smile like she's so happy to see me. I want her to stop looking at me that way. I'll help her and leave.

I want to be sure she still wants my help.

"Tessa, are you sure you're okay with me helping you get undressed?" I choke out because images of her naked body still swirl around in my mind.

Slowly, she reaches a hand up to my cheek, patting it harder than I think she realizes. I feel a slight sting spread through my cheek. "Oh, Lenox. Don't be shy. I'm wearing my good underwear," she explains like that's the only thing I'm worried about when it comes to taking her pants off.

She's so damn cute.

"Well, then, let's get you ready for bed," I smile. "Sit back down. I'll grab your robe off the chair over here."

When we came in, I noticed the robe. This will be perfect because I won't have to dig through her drawers. She sits down as I directed while I grab the robe. I can hear her humming, and when I turn around, she's now trying to yank the shirt she's wearing over her head.

Arms straight up in the air, unable to move anymore; she murmurs from beneath the shirt, "Uh, Lenox? I'm stuck."

This time, I do laugh as I walk over to her.

"Stay still. I've got this," I inform her.

Tessa does exactly what I tell her to do as I lift the shirt over her head. I try to keep my eyes off of her, off the smooth skin of her shoulders, off her perky breasts.

Kneeling in front of her, I pull her jeans, and they move over her hips and down her legs. Her smooth, long, beautiful legs. Oh shit, I need to hurry. Once I have them off, I start to stand up, but Tessa stops me when she twines her fingers through my hair. We're eye level, our gazes locked.

Before I even know what's happening, she pulls my head forward, pressing her lips against mine.

147

My mind racing, I freeze as her lips slowly, gently caress mine. Her lips feel so good. I need to stop this, pull away. But, it just feels so damn good. Better than I imagined. She whispers my name against my lips just before she slides to her knees in front of me, running her hands beneath my shirt. My grip on reality slips the moment she deepens the kiss. Pulling her closer, I take everything she wants to give me.

Almost as quickly as it began, it ends. My mother raised a gentleman, and this isn't very gentlemanly. I lightly grip her shoulders and push her back.

"Tessa, we need to stop. You don't know what you're doing. I'd be an asshole if I let this continue," I state, an edge to my voice because everything in me is at war with the words leaving my mouth.

She gazes at me with a dazed look in her eyes, lips swollen from our kiss. So damn beautiful. Her head dips in a small nod, I reach for the robe lying on the floor next to us, our eyes remaining connected. Pulling the robe over her shoulders, pulling one arm and then the other through the short, silky sleeves.

Once I tie it in front of her, I pull her back against me into a hug. I whisper into her ear, "One day."

Helping her stand, she crawls into her bed, lying down, her small frame swallowed by the down comforter she has on her bed. At the end of the bed, I see a soft cashmere blanket, and I unfold it, laying it across her body. Crawling up next to her, I lean in to place a kiss on the soft skin of her cheek. She's already asleep, her breathing shallow.

Moving off the bed, I turn to the door, and that's when I notice it. Sitting there on her bedside table like it belongs, except it doesn't. I reach for it but stop. What am I doing? I can't take it. It's not mine anymore, in fact, I'm not sure I realized it before now, but I don't want it anymore. For the first time in ten years, I think I want something else.

I walk to the door; stopping to take one last look at the girl on the bed. She's beginning to change my mind. I don't know if she will remember what happened, but I do know one thing. I will never forget what it was like to have Tessa Collins' lips against mine for the first time.

Walking out of Tessa's room, down the hall, and into her living room, I try to wrap my mind around what just happened. The feelings it evoked within me. I want to ask her what she felt. I want to know if it was just the alcohol or if it was something more. The same kind of more that I'm feeling. So many questions, very little answers.

I look around the room. It's just like I imagined. Tessa's simplistic beauty. Tidy and minimal, her built-in bookshelves the only thing filled to the point that nothing else will fit. When I walk to the shelf, I read the titles which are all in alphabetical order by author. Most I have not heard of, and when I pull one out, I almost laugh at loud at the irony that most of them appear to be romance novels. Romance. Ha. The girl who doesn't believe in romance has bookshelves full of love stories.

As my eyes continue to roam over the titles, I notice a picture album stuck on the bottom shelf.

Maybe I should feel sorry for snooping, but I'm not hurting anything. I've decided to stay a little while so I can make sure Tessa is okay and doesn't wake up feeling sick. While I wait, it won't hurt to flip through her photo album.

Pulling it off the shelf, I walk over to her couch, sitting down and opening the album. My eyes drift over every page like it's the most interesting story ever. The story of Tessa. In this book, I find baby Tessa, toddler Tessa, and so on. I get a glimpse into what kind of life Tessa has led all the way to the present. Everything indicates that Tessa has had a happy life, it seems her parents are still married and very much in love if these pictures are any indication. So if her life has been so filled with love, what holds her back?

Putting the photo album on the table, I notice a book sitting there. A bookmark is sticking out of the top. Curious, I pick it up and read the title, Archer's Voice.

Opening it up, I decide to see exactly what is so romantic about

Archer's voice.

Soft lips touching mine wakes me. When I open my eyes, I'm staring into cornflower blue eyes shining with amusement. At first, I'm a little startled by their presence, but it feels like the lips currently pressed against my lips were meant only for mine.

Involuntarily my arms wrap around her as she crawls up into my lap. She fits perfectly.

"Good morning," Tessa breathes in between kisses. "I'm so glad you stayed."

"Me, too," I reveal, startled when she takes my bottom lip in between hers.

We continue to devour one another with our mouths, unable to get close enough, pulling at one another, until I flip her on her back and hover over her. My hand caresses the side of her face as I look into her eyes, "Tessa, you're so beautiful. I wanted you last night, but I'm glad we waited because now I know you want me, too."

A smile spreads across her face, eyes shimmering.

"Lenox, I'm so glad I found you," she practically whispers. "I knew the moment I read your words that I had to be with you. I know you're the one who's been writing those letters to me. I'm so glad it's you and only you."

I lean down, kissing her along her collar bone as she moans in pleasure. She isn't mad at me that I kept this from her. She's known all along and still wants me.

"Tessa...Tessa...Tessa," I keep repeating her name quietly as my lips claim every part of her, my eyes closed, only the familiar lilac scent letting me know Tessa is here with me.

Suddenly, she's saying my name, but something doesn't sound right. Her voice doesn't sound like she is feeling the same pleasure I am. In fact, her voice seems distant and confused.

When I open my eyes, Tessa is standing over me, eyes wide in confusion.

"Lenox?" she says as she pulls her floral silk robe tighter around her.

Blinking, I try to gain my composure.

"Lenox, what are you doing here? Did you sleep on my couch?" Suddenly, her lip quirks up in one corner. "Did you fall asleep on my couch reading *Archer's Voice*?"

She looks like she wants to laugh all the while my insides feel as if they're hanging out for her to stomp on.

It was all just a dream.

November 1, 2014

Sara just told me she'll be gone for Thanksgiving this year. She said it was a work thing. A convention that will keep her out of town until the day before Thanksgiving and due to holiday travel, getting a flight home is impossible. We haven't spent a Thanksgiving apart in 9 years. I told her I understood. I told her I love her. She said, "me too." Only me too. I'm still holding on, but I can't help but wonder if Sara is still holding on, too.

CHAPTER 22

TESSA

WHEN I WALK OUT OF my room and into the living area, I nearly scream. A full head of hair is peeking just above the side of the couch. Who is that? I think really hard about what I did last night as I tiptoe over to the sofa to peer at the stranger on my couch.

Once I reach the couch, I let out a quiet gasp. Lenox.

He looks so peaceful sleeping with an open book lying on his chest. I smile because he was reading *Archer's Voice*. It's not exactly a typical guy's book. What is he doing here anyway? I take the opportunity to watch him sleep. He really is handsome. I can still imagine the sharp line of his jaw beneath his beard. It's really unfair how beautiful he looks with his eyelashes sweeping his cheeks. They're so long.

Is he mumbling something in his sleep? My name? Lenox must be dreaming, and part of me wants desperately to know what he is dreaming about right now as my name leaves his lips again. The thought makes the butterflies in my stomach flutter.

Nudging his leg with my barefoot, I call his name softly, "Lenox?"

His eyes open, blinking rapidly while he tries to focus on what is happening.

"Lenox, what are you doing here? Did you sleep on my couch?" I ask him, trying hard to hide my smile. "Did you fall asleep on my couch reading *Archer's Voice?*"

I wait for him to answer me.

He rubs the sleep out of his eyes, yawning before he answers, "Okay, that's a lot of questions before I have my coffee, but I'm going to give them a shot." His lips move in an upward turn. "I'm here because I brought you home last night. I only meant to stay a little while until I knew you were alright, and you weren't going to be sick. I fell asleep, and yes, *Archer's Voice* was so soothing that it put me right to sleep."

He's such a smartass.

"You're so weird," I say as I roll my eyes. "Do you want some coffee?" I offer, leaving him sitting on the couch while I head for the kitchen.

"Sure. I take it black," he calls after me.

As I pull a couple of coffee pods from the cabinet, I grimace when I realize I'm only wearing a robe with my bra and panties beneath it. Great, Tessa. Just great. Well, it's too late now. I wonder just how much of me he has seen.

When both cups are made, I carry them into the living room determined to find out just how far things went last...

I stop dead in my tracks. Last night—the memory of the whole night rushed back to me.

"Oh, fuck," I groan, my voice echoing through the room, my face immediately turning what I am sure is the brightest and deepest shade of red known to humanity.

Lenox is standing now, looking directly at me, a grin on his face.

"What?" he asks me, but I can tell by the look on his face he

155

knows exactly why that particular four letter word just came out of my mouth.

"Lenox, be honest with me, but did I throw myself at you last night?" He is directly in front of me now, and he takes his cup of coffee from me.

Taking a sip, he sighs, "Look, Tessa, you did kiss me, but I kissed you right back. I was wrong, and I'm so so sorry."

Now I'm confused; why is he apologizing to me? I practically attacked him. He has no reason to apologize.

"Don't be sorry! It was me, I'm sorry, I don't normally do that kind of thing," I blurt out, sloshing my coffee in the process.

Lenox takes my coffee and places it on the table then sets his next to it before he grips me gingerly by the shoulders. Forcing me to look him in the eyes because up to this point I've been trying to avoid direct eye contact.

"Tessa, don't apologize. It wasn't unwanted. Hell, I'm just glad I came to my senses. You're hurting my ego by apologizing because it sucks thinking you only kissed me because you were a little intoxicated. I'd prefer you completely sober, but I'm glad you did it."

My heart races and those damn butterflies are really flapping their wings now.

He leans in and lightly kisses the corner of my mouth. My ability to breathe vanishes. His lips linger for a moment before he pulls back.

"I really like you, Tessa Collins. You do something to me, and I look forward to finding out just what that might be," he confesses.

I'm at a loss for words. My ability to form a simple reply is nonexistent. I can only look deep into his crystal blue eyes, searching them for something to indicate this is all just a game. I only see the truth.

Lenox holds my gaze then drops his hands. "I've got to go if I want to make it home to change before work," he tells me. Picking up my hand, he places a light kiss on the ends of my fingers.

He walks away, my eyes following him to the door, trying to

decipher every emotion he just stirred inside me. I remain silent.

Just before he walks out of the door, he turns back to me, a serious look on his face. "Oh and Tessa?" He pauses before continuing, "You were right."

What does that mean? I'm right? I look at him questioningly.

Finally, I speak. "About what?"

His eyes light up, shining as he says, "You were right; you were wearing your good underwear."

With that, he walks through the doorway and closes the door behind him. Leaving me staring after him, in my living room, in nothing but my robe, lace bra, and my good underwear.

I haven't been able to get Lenox off my mind all morning so it didn't help one bit when I walk into my office that Chad was sitting behind my desk waiting for me to arrive.

"Buttercup, give me the dirty flirty details and don't leave anything out," he trills.

I roll my eyes, setting my belongings down on the credenza to the left of my desk.

"Nothing," I lie, knowing my response will never be good enough for Chad. He's going to pry and pry until I spill every last detail.

After Lenox had left, I ran the night before through my head. I remember every detail of what kissing him, touching him felt like and what it did to me. I clung to him like I was dying of thirst and he was my last drink of water. I've never felt that kind of passion.

"Tess, don't you dare lie to me and don't try to deny it. I see it written on your face. Something happened with that hot specimen of a man last night, and now you're scared shitless," he chides.

Sitting in the chair on the opposite side of my desk, I flop down.

"Fine, but do not read more into it than it is, Chad Borchgardt," I insist, wagging my finger in his direction. He just rolls his eyes and crosses his arms over his chest as if he's insulted. "Okay, he took me home since I was a bit tipsy so to speak." He rolls his eyes again. I ignore him, continuing, "He walked me upstairs." I begin to talk faster as if it will keep Chad from hearing the rest of my confession. "And helped me get to bed and stayed the night."

I avoid eye contact with him, which is a bad idea and only makes things worse. Why must I always do things to perpetuate these things in Chad's mind. The more I avoid, the more he assumes.

I shift my eyes in his direction. He's staring at me, his mouth slightly agape.

"It's not what it sounds like," I say defensively.

"Uh, huh," he replies as if he doesn't believe me. "I don't doubt that, actually, Tessa, because I know you." Before I can say anything, Chad puts his hand in the air to stop me. "BUT, I also know there's more to it than you're saying, too. So spill."

"I hate you," I tell him before giving him the full truth. "He helped me, and I basically threw myself at him. Shit, Chad. I kissed him when I was in nothing but my bra and panties. I ran my hands under his shirt, touching his well-muscled back and would have kept going if he hadn't stopped me. I'm mortified," I confess. "I didn't fully recall everything until he was walking out of my door and made some teasing remark to me."

I can't read his face. He's watching me and thinking. I recognize that face.

Finally, he speaks. "First, I'm so incredibly proud of you," he says, and I'm about to tell him he's nuts, but he continues, "Second, I have only one question. Did he kiss you back before he stopped it from going further?"

Confused, I ask him, "What does that have to do with anything?"

Rolling his eyes at me for the millionth time since we walked into my office, he says, "Just answer the question, Tessa."

"Well, yes, but I didn't give him much choice," I argue.

"Oh, buttercup, there's always a choice," he assures me. "He's apparently a gentleman. Don't take that personally and don't be embarrassed, because he wanted it, too." His face begins to glow. "I think he's worth every bit of your time, and just may hold up to my standards for you."

"Your standards? You've set me up with hundreds of jerks," I exclaim.

Chad looks over at me. "Honey, you have to kiss the frogs to find the prince."

My phone rings and a burst of laughter leaves my lips as I lift the phone to my ear. "Hello."

"Well, you sound happy," the voice on the other end of the line says. "I'm going to take that as a good sign you're not upset with me about last night."

Lenox. My palms begin to sweat. I feel nervous. My God, why do I feel so nervous? I look at Chad, eyes wide. "Lenox," I mouth to him.

His face lights up, and he quickly stands, slipping out of my office.

"Uh, Tessa? Have I lost you?" Lenox says through the phone.

"Oh. Oh, yes. I'm sorry. I'm here," I stutter out. "Of course, I'm not upset with you. Who knows what would have happened if you hadn't helped me through the door?"

He laughs, a deep, low sound echoing through the phone. "Yeah, that's a scary thought." He pauses then says, "Since you're feeling so good. Would it be presumptuous of me to think you might let me take you to dinner tonight?"

The fluttering feeling in my stomach kicks in high gear. I really like Lenox Malone.

"No," I say.

"Okay, no, I'm not presumptuous or no, you won't go to dinner with me?"

"No, not presumptuous," I clarify.

"Good, I'll pick you up at seven thirty?" he suggests.

"Seven thirty is perfect," I reply.

"Have a good day, Tessa Collins," he says.

"You too," I say just before I hang up.

Yes, I definitely like Lenox Malone, and that's what scares me most.

Walking side by side, his hand brushes mine, not once, but twice. When I glance at him from the corner of my eye, his head is facing forward, a look of subtle contentment on his face. His hand brushes mine again, but this time, he lightly takes my hand in his gentle grasp.

A giggle slips out; I can't help myself.

Stopping, Lenox pulls me around. "What's so funny?"

"You're just so smooth, Malone," I laugh.

He watches me, his facial expression is unchanging, but I can see something in his eyes that sends a shiver up my spine. Whatever it is, he decides not to share it with me. He's holding it back. I wonder why, but before I can think too long about it, he tightens his grip, and we continue walking.

"Can I ask where we're going?" I ask after a few minutes.

"Well, I hope you don't mind, but I have dinner packed in my bag. I thought it might be fun to be outside on this warm fall evening. I was thinking of going to Republic Square and sitting under the old oak tree," he answers, adjusting the strap of his bag at the same time, drawing my attention to it.

"No, not at all," I approve. It's a sweet idea. In fact, I'd prefer this to yelling across a table to be heard in a crowded restaurant.

As we approach the limestone area under the magnificent oak tree, Lenox chooses one of the many small round bistro tables for us to sit and begins removing things from the bag he was carrying. Although it's a warm night, there's a slight breeze blowing through the tops of the trees. Looking around us, we are the only people here. The night is beautiful. I feel happy. It's been a long time since I've felt this good.

I feel a light touch at the base of my back. Turning, I find a smiling Lenox. He's so close I want to lean in and place my lips on his soft mouth. I don't though. Instead, I return his smile.

"Let's sit down. I hope you're hungry," he remarks as he pulls my chair out for me to take a seat.

The small table has a single tea light sitting in the middle of it surrounded by several take out Chinese boxes. Immediately, Lenox takes a seat and offers me the choice of chopsticks or a fork.

"I wasn't sure which you would use," he says.

Reaching for the chopsticks, I grin at the approval I saw in his eyes.

"Also, I thought I'd let you pick what you want, and we'd just use the boxes instead of plates," he pauses, eyes twinkling before he continues. "I got a little of everything."

He's doing all the talking; I've yet to say anything. Lenox seems as nervous as I feel on the inside. It's charming.

"Thank you," I finally say. "This is sweet and Chinese food is my favorite."

I pick up the kung pao chicken, dipping my chopsticks in, and taking a bite. He watches me, smiles, then picks up the chow mein. We eat in silence for a while, and the best part is it isn't awkward. We're just enjoying the moment, something I haven't done in a long time.

"Tell me something about Lenox Malone you think I should know," I say, interrupting our silence. I like the way I can read his feelings by the change of expression on his face. He likes I want to know about him. I like the idea that he wants me to know him.

Lenox taps his finger to his chin, pretending he's thinking hard about what he wants to divulge.

"I was raised by the greatest single mom on the planet, so I'm a bit spoiled," he says, raising an eyebrow like I might challenge his confession in some way.

A burst of laughter escapes me, "that's the one thing I should know about you?"

Grinning, he takes another bite of food. "Yep, It's the first thing, at least."

"The first thing?" There's something about the way he said "first thing" that tells me there's more.

"Tessa, there's lots of things you should know about me…and things I hope to know about you. I figure I'd start at the beginning," he explains. "So it's your turn, tell me something about Tessa Collins I should know."

"Okay, well…" I start. "I'm a helper. I enjoy helping people which is why I work at the shelter. It's always been my dream, and sometimes I wonder if staying here in Austin is enough," I say, honestly.

I'm not sure why I say that, but it speaks volumes about me. I've never told anyone that before, but for some reason, I thought telling Lenox would be safe. He watches me without saying a word. I beg him silently not to ask more of my confession. I can see he wants to but changes his mind.

"Your turn," I add quickly before he changes his mind again.

"I love cats," he states. "I love their fickle affection. One minute they adore you and want all of your love then the next they want you to leave them alone. I find their independence fascinating."

This time, I laugh so hard and loud, I can't control myself. The most content look rests on his face as he watches me, he likes the idea that I find him ridiculous and funny. He loves that he makes me laugh.

When I finally stop laughing, I ask, "Do you have a cat?"

"Yes, his name is Roosevelt. He is most fickle of all," he smirks. "You're up."

"I'm a romance novel junkie," I admit. "I read at least two to three a week if time allows."

"Oh, yes. I noticed. I don't blame you, that Archer is dreamy," he teases.

I'd forgotten I found him with my book opened on his chest, fast asleep this morning.

"Are you making fun of me?"

"No, not at all. I'm only sorry I fell asleep before I finished the book," he explains, a broad grin on his face.

"You can borrow it, anytime," I tease.

We continue our back and forth. Teasing one another, laughing, and getting to know one another bit by bit. The wall being chipped away a little at a time. Lenox Malone is pushing his way in, and I'm not sure I can stop him.

April 24, 2015

I'm sitting in Faulk Central Library heartbroken. I came here for peace. For quiet. To clear my mind. Sara ended things a month ago, and I've been trying to come up with some way to win her back. How do I stop loving her? I've loved her for ten years. Ten Years. She said she just couldn't do it anymore. I haven't been able to think of a way to win her back or a way to stop loving her. Until now. I'm not going to love anymore. I'm not holding on anymore.

Goodbye, Sara.

CHAPTER 23

Lenox

MY EYELIDS FLY OPEN. A loud banging sound is echoing through my house. It takes me a minute to realize someone is at my front door. Reaching over, I grab my phone from the side table, the screen lights up, letting me know it's nine in the morning.

Who is at my door at nine in the morning?

Throwing back the covers, I stretch my arms over my head, taking my time. Whoever it is can wait. The banging picks back up again, only louder this time. Damn it; I know it's Sammy. He's the only one rude enough to continue beating on the door when no one answers it right away instead of assuming the person is not home or still asleep.

Stalking to the door, I throw it open. Yep, I was right. Sammy is standing on my front porch, a scowl on his face, and hand mid-air about to begin another assault on my door.

"Dude, it's early," I complain as I open the door wider, allowing him in.

166

Shooting me the finger, he walks past me through the door.

"Well, if you had returned my call yesterday after walking out on me Thursday night at the club, I wouldn't be tracking you down," he argues back. "Speaking of walking out on me, what are the fucking odds you'd run into that girl again?"

Again? Confused, I try to let what Sammy just said roll around in my head. Maybe I'm still half asleep because I would swear he said run into her again.

"Did you just say, again?" I ask him in case I did hear him wrong.

Walking into my kitchen, he opens the fridge, searching for something to eat. Sammy has no problem making himself right at home.

As he takes an enormous bite out of my leftover sub sandwich, he nods his head. "Yep, she's that girl you ran into on the street a couple of months ago. You know, we were beer wasted, and you were being a dick and forgot to call the Uber."

I know the particular night he's talking about because I got pissed off at him for pulling me in the car. It was also the night I was reeling over that first post it note Tessa left on my door, although I didn't know it was her at the time. The girl. I felt something. She smelled of lilac.

"Are you saying the woman I left with the other night is the same girl? How can you know that? You were just as drunk as I was that night," I question him, still doubting.

"I was drunk, not blind. She's hot," he tells me, a mouth full of sandwich. "I wouldn't forget that face."

Walking over to the couch, I take a seat. "Holy, fuck," I mutter, running my hands over my face and through my hair. Looking up at Sammy, I ask, "Are you sure?" Even as I ask the question, her scent comes back to me. The familiarity of it. The one I recognized, but couldn't place.

"Nox, what the fuck? Why are you acting so weird?" He asks, shaking his head. "Yes, I'm sure," he confirms again as he takes a seat next to me.

"Sam, I didn't realize it was the same girl. I was so drunk that night; I could barely see straight," I explain. "When I left you, I only knew I was leaving with Tessa. Tessa Collins, the girl who found my journal. The girl I've been writing letters to for the last month."

Sammy slaps me on the back, knocking me forward. "Dude, no way!" He exclaims. "What are the odds? Are you serious?"

"Dead serious," I affirm.

"That's some kismet type shit going on right there," he says, leaning back and making himself more comfortable.

Jesus. I'd seen Tessa before I actually saw her. I was drawn to her before I even knew her. I don't believe in meant to be. I stopped believing a long time ago. This whole situation gives me an uneasy feeling, yet it all makes some sort of odd sense. It makes the idea of my immediate attraction to her all the more complicated. I wonder if she knows, if my memory is correct, she noticed me that night, too. But, if she knew then why wouldn't she just say something. Standing up, I pace the room. She hasn't said anything because she doesn't know.

This is all too weird. Too much.

"You're making me nervous. Sit down," Sammy proposes. "Why do you look scared shitless? I think this is great, why don't you?"

Staring at him, I try to think of the best way to explain what I'm feeling.

"Sam, this is all happening too fast. The girl, the feelings she brings up for me, the pull of her. I'm going to scare her, hell I'm scaring myself. I swore I'd never do this again," I admit to him as I continue to pace.

"Nox, this isn't Sara. Fast or slow, haven't you preached to me since we hit puberty that taking a risk is worth it?" He leans forward, putting his elbows on his knees. "I think that was the worst part of the aftermath of Sara, watching you give up. It's not in you, Nox. Quit fighting it, man."

God, I hate when Sammy makes sense. It's fucking annoying.

He stands up, walking over to me; he places his hand on my shoulder. "If it feels right then go for it. Did you tell her, yet?"

I know he's right, looking over at him I shake my head, no.

"Nox, man, you need to tell her before she finds out. Quit trying to save yourself before you even take the leap," Sammy tells me. He starts to leave, stopping as he reaches the front door. Looking over his shoulder, he says, "Oh yeah, you might wanna call your hot mama. I left her a message about you not answering my calls for a full day. She'll be worried."

He opens the door and is gone before I can punch him for calling my mom hot and for worrying her.

The purring sound of my soft fluffy cat rubbing against my leg grabs my attention. I bend down, picking Roosevelt up, pulling him close. He willingly allows it. It must be one of his free passes to love days. "Roosevelt, I wish I was as good as you are at turning my emotions on and off," I confess. He purrs louder when I pull him closer. "I've got to find a way to tell Tessa about the letters without scaring her away." I'm not sure I'm ready to tell her just yet.

Just how long can I put this off?

As I shut off the water and step out of the shower, I hear a familiar voice call my name. Apparently, my mom is early. Or am I running late? I definitely didn't want to get out after my nearly ten-mile run this morning; the water felt good pelting my muscles.

I call to her as I dry off. "Sorry, Mom. I'll be out in a few minutes. I ran farther than I intended today."

"No problem, honey," she shouts back.

Pulling on a pair of jeans and a t-shirt, I make my way down the hall and into the living room.

She's sitting on the couch and as usual, Roosevelt is curled up next to her. The one and the only person that cat is devoted to is my mom. Little asshole, what a traitor. I'm the one who rescued him.

"Hey, sweetie," she says when she sees me. She continues to flip through the magazine in her lap.

Leaning down, I place a kiss on her cheek. "Hey. I'm sorry Sam worried you," I apologize as I walk into the kitchen for some water.

"Man, sometimes I think that boy worries about you more than I do," she snorts. "I don't mind though because it gave me an excuse to call you and take you to lunch."

"Mom, you know you don't have to make up an excuse to call. I like when you call me, and even more, I like when you take me to lunch," I joke, winking at her when I walk back in the room.

"Aha! I knew it; you only use me for food. I suspected as much your whole life," she teases back.

I plop down next to her on the couch, Roosevelt lifts his head and throws daggers at me with his eyes as if I'm interrupting something. I ignore him, leaning into my mom, needing a little comfort. I don't care how old I get; she always makes me feel better.

"Lenox, what's on your mind?" she asks me.

"How do you always know?" I answer her question with a question.

She pats me on the leg. "Oh, honey, I'm your mother. I always know when you need to talk about something."

"I'm not even sure I can explain this to you," I tell her. "This girl, she has me in knots. I'm tangled up in her from so many directions, Mom. I don't know how to trust it. She has no idea either."

"Lenox, one of the best things about you is your incredibly huge heart. You can't hide from the person you are. This is not Sara." She pauses a moment to let her words sink in. Taking my hand in hers, she continues, "Do you hear what I'm saying? You've been lucky to have loved someone so beautifully once, but from what I hear in your voice, you think you have the opportunity to have a great love again. Don't let it pass you by out of fear, Lenox because that would be the tragedy, not the possibility of heartache."

The surprising thing about my mother is no matter how life has tried to beat her down; she's never lost her ability to find the positive side of its disappointments. She keeps fighting, never gives up.

"Have you given up on love, Mom?" I ask her. We've never discussed why she never married or really dated. It has always been the two of us. When she wasn't focused solely on me, then she was focused on school. "You're young, and you deserved to be happy."

Placing her hand over mine, she sighs, "I am happy, Lenox. You make me happy. My work makes me happy. I've loved Lenox, and I'm not opposed to loving again. If I found that person who sends chills over my skin and makes my insides tingle then I would grab on and never let go."

"I love you, Mom," I tell her.

"I love you too, Lenox," she says softly. "You know what you want, so take it. Be honest with her. You'll work it out, maybe try writing again."

Leaning farther into her, I embrace her comfort and advice.

"Write? Yeah, maybe I will," I decide.

Lying in bed, I stare up at the ceiling, unable to fall asleep. My date the night before playing through my mind, along with the conversations with both Sammy and my mother.

It all comes down to the fact that I do like Tessa.

There's something about her that reaches some inner part of me. I owe it to myself and her to find out where this all leads. She found my journal for a reason. Our lives keep crossing paths, and it's worth the risk to find out why.

I'm just not sure falling in love is something I can risk.

I'll just take this slow. We'll go out more; I'll keep writing her and find a way to confess to her how we're truly connected. I want to be sure she's on the same page as me because, after only a few dates, I can feel myself starting to lose my balance when it comes to her.

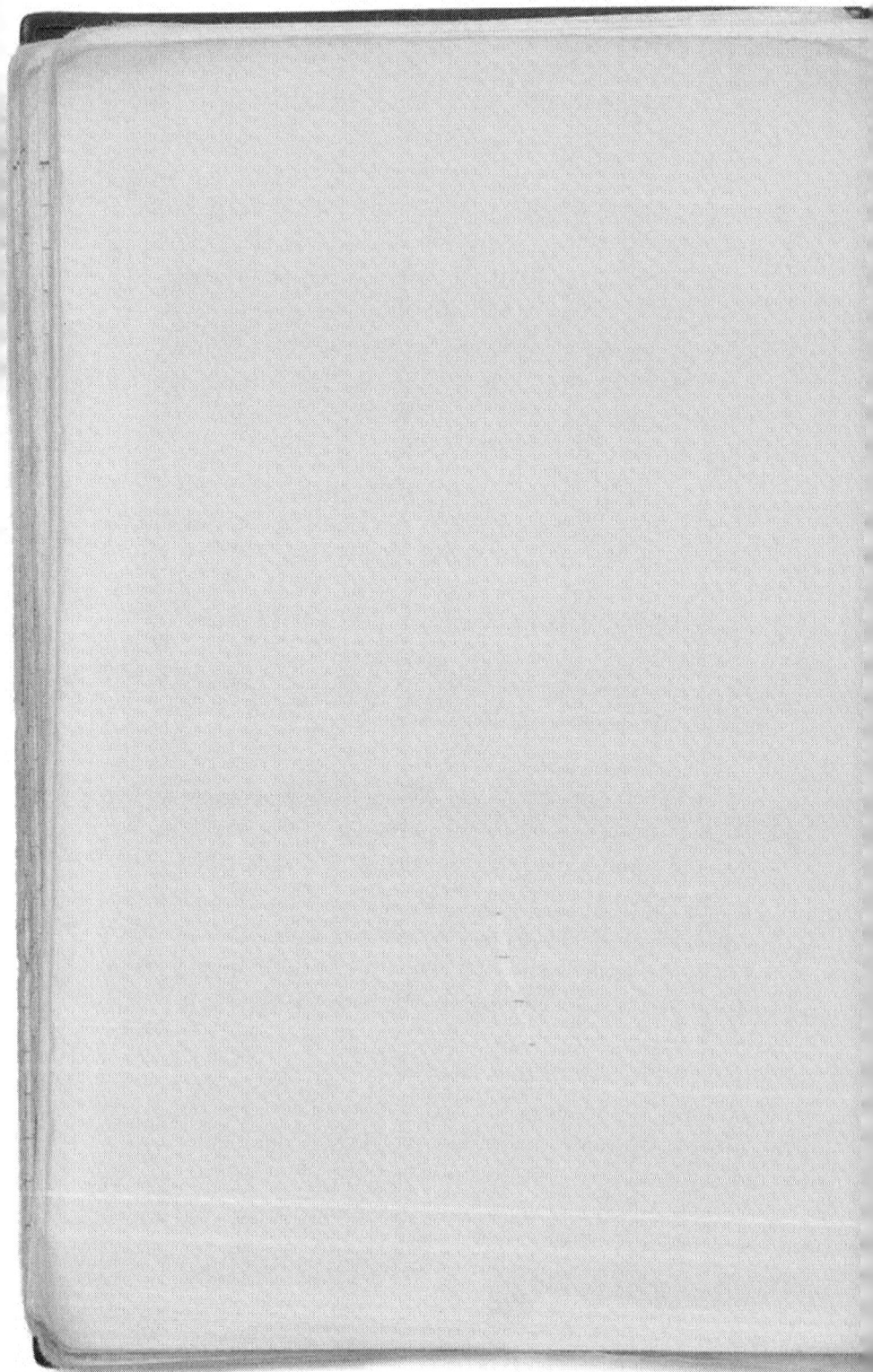

CHAPTER 24

Lenox

A FEW DAYS HAVE PASSED since my date with Tessa and the conversations I had with Sammy and my mom. I've had time for things to settle in my mind. Tessa and I have spoken a couple of times a day and decided to have lunch tomorrow. When I hear her voice something inside me wants to reach out to her and hold on, take the risk, forget everything but the way she makes me feel. Because Tessa Collins definitely makes me feel.

As I walk into the house and over to the bar between my kitchen and living room, I notice a wrapped package on it that wasn't there this morning when I left for work.

Picking it up, I unwrap it slowly.

Shaking my head with a grin, I read the note stuck to the front of the book.

Lenox,

You've always found your answers when you write your thoughts down. Writing is a part of the man you've always been, es-

pecially writing about how you feel. I think it's because you feel so much, more than most people. You can't change that about yourself because it's who you are. I know I'm your mother, but I love who you are. You deserve to have everything you want so take some time and decide if this girl is who you want...she could be so lucky. I bought you your first journal so you could pour all those emotions I could see hiding inside you into it when you were only sixteen, that hasn't changed. Embrace it, figure out what you want, and if it's this girl, hold on tight and never let go.

Love always,
Mom

She's right about the journal. She's usually right about everything so maybe I just need to breathe and focus on what Tessa makes me feel. Trust myself. Once I trust myself then maybe I can trust her.

Walking down the hall into my room, I lay the journal down on my desk. I pull out my phone and quickly send my mom a text.

Lenox: *Thanks for the push, Kristin.*
Mom: *You're welcome, and you're still not old enough to call me by my first name, so stop.*

Laughing out loud, I tap in my response.

Lenox: *Yes, Momma. I love you.*
Mom: *Love you too, baby. Be kind to yourself. You deserve it. xoxo*
Lenox: *xo*

Setting my phone down next to my bed, I begin to get undressed. I'm exhausted from the day and need to relax. Once I get changed, I pick up the dark blue notebook, carry it into the living room, and take a seat next to Roosevelt, who purrs quietly to acknowledge me.

I open it up to the first page, scribble the date at the top then begin to open up to the emotions needing a release. Moving forward. Moving on.

I watch the way her eyes light up as she laughs and how her cheek dimples on one side when she's trying not to smile at something I say. I'm noticing the little things today. Analyzing every moment of silence, every glance in my direction, trying to imagine what Tessa is thinking. I want to know how she is feeling.

"You know, I've never asked, and you've never said, do you have siblings?" Her question interrupts my thoughts.

"I'm an only child. It's always been just my mom and me," I tell her.

"Your dad?" She seems to ask reluctantly.

"I've never met him. When my mom found out she was pregnant, he left. They were very young, and he wasn't ready. I've never tried to find him, although my mom hasn't discouraged it. My mom is pretty special. I always felt the love she gave me was enough. She's strong and smart. She has a unique gift of taking care of people, which is why she probably became a nurse," I reveal. "Honestly, I've never felt compelled to find him. My mom has always been enough."

She has a thoughtful look on her face, her eyes never leaving mine. I'm thankful I don't see pity on her face. I've always hated when people feel sorry for me when it comes to the man who helped give me life. There is none on Tessa's face; I only see a sort of admiration I'm not used to seeing. The look she is giving me creates a warm sensation in my chest.

"What about you?" I ask her, hoping to avoid the feeling.

"Well, I'm also an only child. My parents waited ten years to have me," she explains. "They're incredible parents. My mom and dad have always let me live my life the way I've wanted; supported my dreams."

I want to know Tessa's dreams.

Leaning in closer to her, unable to hold back, I ask her, "What are your dreams?"

Her face brightens. "I want to make an impact on the world even if it's only a small sliver. I want to be happy and find love, have a family, the usual. My parents have been married for thirty-five years; that's a lot to live up to for a girl."

I can hear a sadness and doubt in the way she said those words. "What do you mean by that?" I can't help but ask.

Head turned down; she's picking at the polish on her nails. I repeat my question, needing to know the answer. "Tessa, what do you mean by that?"

Lifting her gaze slowly to mine, she remains silent for a moment like she's searching for the right words. She still seems unsure when she says, "I'm not sure that kind of love is possible for everyone…for me. I'm afraid of getting it wrong."

Tessa is afraid to fail at love. This is why she doesn't believe in romance and love. My heart aches because she deserves to have her dreams come true.

Reaching my hand across the table, I cover hers with mine. Her eyes meet mine again.

In barely a whisper, I say, "Don't be scared."

When I get home that night, I go to my desk and pull out the sticky notes Tessa has left for me.

Our conversation at lunch today was stuck on repeat in my mind the rest of the afternoon. I know Sammy recognized I was distracted, but for once he kept his mouth shut and left me alone.

Today she revealed a small part of why she struggles with believing in love and romance even if it doesn't entirely make sense to me.

Laying them in front of me, I begin to read her words. I'm trying to determine if she leaves any clues as to how I might convince her to see it can and will happen to her. It's going on right now or so

I think it is. I feel like there is something between us, we just need to reach out and grab it.

She asked me to tell her why I'm writing her these letters. What loves means to me? Why did I stop believing?

I don't even know if I can answer her. Am I capable of letting go and taking this risk? Are my wants for Tessa and the possibilities of what we could be together greater than my fear of losing myself?

I need to answer these questions for myself, so I can give her the answers she needs.

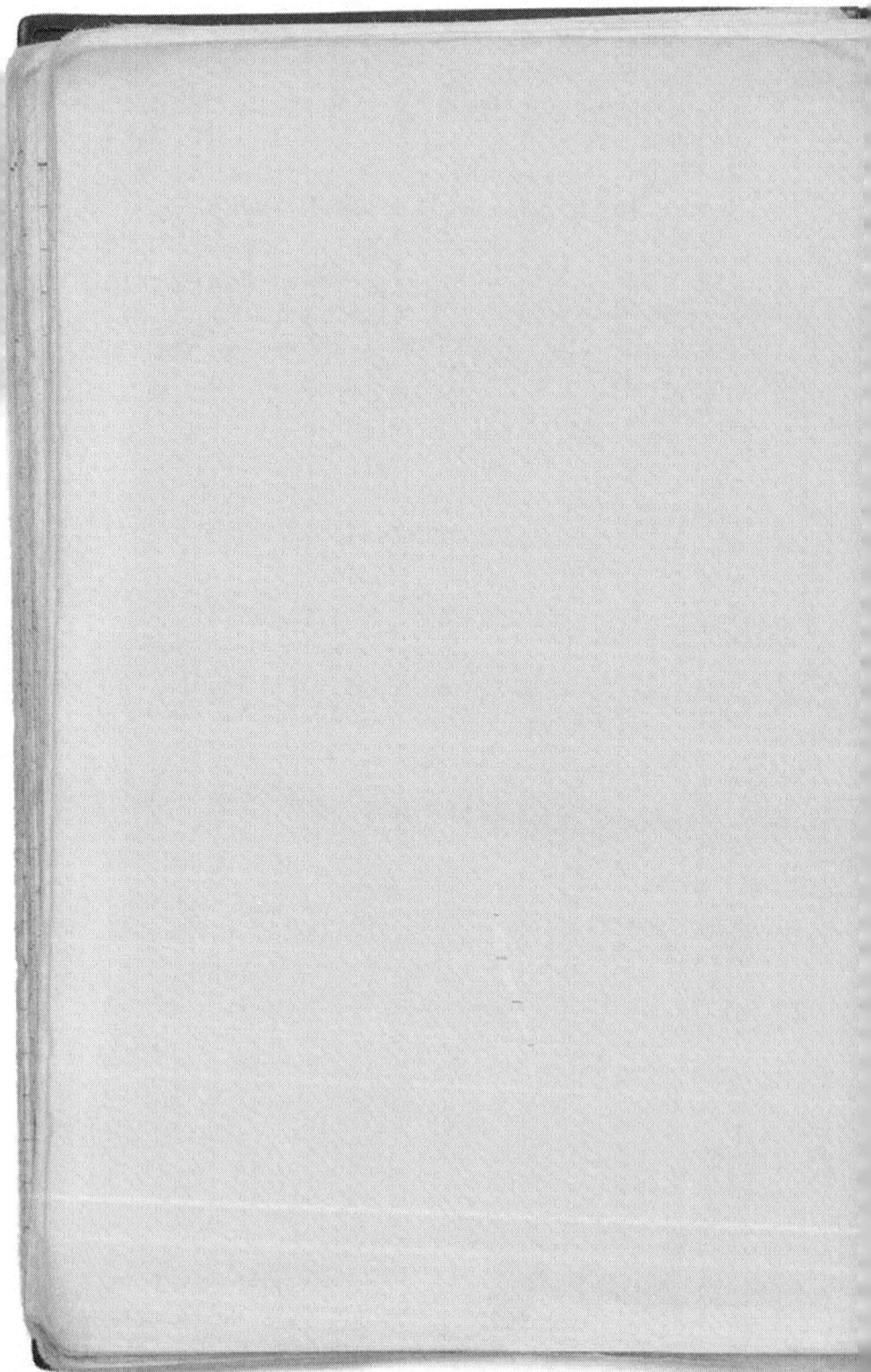

CHAPTER 25

TESSA

THE LAST WEEK HAS BEEN a whirlwind. Between work and lunch dates and a couple of dinner dates, my schedule has been on overload, and I've had little time to think. Every moment I spend with Lenox is so easy, but I still hold back. I'm not sure I know how to take the chance.

Then there are these letters, like the one I'm holding in my hand. Letters. They are only letters; only words from a stranger yet I feel something so strong when I pick them up from my desk and read the words written just for me. The words aren't life-altering in any way, but they are genuine and obviously written from the heart. For those reasons alone, I find them romantic.

Slipping the letter opener into the envelope, I open it and pull out the letter, taking a deep breath before I let my eyes drift over the words.

Tessa,

I'll get the easy stuff out of the way. My favorite color is blue. A soft color of blue you only see in nature. Many things make me smile, for instance, children's laughter, my mother's love, and rainy days. Honestly, when I thought about that question, I realized there are so many things I could never name them all.

You asked me what made my heart race. The accidental brush of the hand of the girl I love with mine. A gentle kiss on my cheek to wake me in the morning from my lover. Meeting someone new and discovering the possibility of love. Falling in love. They're all simple, but the simple things are what sends my heart into a frenzy. Especially, falling in love.

My first thought when I read your question about why I stopped believing in love was to blame my broken, disappointed heart. I wanted to blame it on allowing myself to be vulnerable to another person. Yes, it may be all those reasons, but if I'm honest it's because I've been trying to deny who I am deep inside. I'm the guy who believes in love. The one who wants love and romance. Recently, I discovered I just might be willing to fall in love again. So while I can't answer why I decided to write these letters to you, I can tell you it was the right thing to do.

You called to me. I heard your heart in the words you spoke that day, and I think now I realize you were searching for me. Or maybe I was searching for you. I think we'll know when it's time for us to move past these letters, but, for now, let's be open to what these letters can offer us.

A way to take the steps we both fear to take. Tessa, just know as strange as this may all seem, it's real.

Falling,

Me

Setting the letter down, I lean back in my chair and close my eyes. There is something in his words that is calling to me, too. My mind is filled with the words of one man and the actions of another. I can't compare them. I can't choose between what I'm beginning to feel for either. I've possibly been wrong all along. Love might be a possibility.

I can't help but feel pulled in two different directions. Maybe Chad is right; I don't have to choose right now

As I walk back into the building from my lunch break, I'm greeted by a smiling familiar face. Although it looks different than the first time I saw him, I wouldn't forget the way the light within shines in the depths of his eyes. He represented every aspect of why I love my job.

"Larry," I greet him with a hug. There is no hesitation from him, and he wraps his arms around me in a friendly embrace. "It's so great to see you. You look incredible," I continue.

Seeing Larry after three months, looking healthy and thriving is exactly why I do what I do. It was what I was trying to explain to Lenox the other day when I told him about my dreams. They're coming true. I'm helping people. Changing their lives, so if this dream is possible then maybe my other dreams are possible, too. The thought causes flutters in my stomach.

"I owe it all to you," he insists. "You helped change my life."

That one simple statement brings a tear to my eye.

"I only help steer you in the right direction. You're the one who made the choices. You're the one who took the chance on yourself. I believed in you, but you believed, too," I affirm.

It's never easy to take a risk of anything kind.

"Well, it helped knowing I had someone like you on my side," he maintains. "I don't want to keep you and I have to get back to work. I just wanted to stop by and say thank you."

Leaning toward him, I give him another hug.

"Thank you, Larry. Take care of yourself and please stop by anytime," I say with sincerity.

When we push back, Larry has a kind look on his face; he promises to stop by again soon. As I watch him leave, I once again remember the conversation I shared with Lenox. The way I felt telling him about my dreams so full of doubt when in reality this moment with Larry is proof that my dreams can and are coming true.

Between the letters and time I've spent with Lenox, there just might be hope for the future I want.

Sitting in my car out in front of his house, I read over the sticky notes I wrote out before I left the office today. I analyze everything I say. A part of me wants to find out where this is going and why this all started. I also feel a little guilty because of Lenox, but I owe it to myself to find out. A part of me knows I'm meant to keep this unusual relationship going.

I'll read it one last time to be sure I've said what I wanted to say; then I'll leave it for him to find. Him. I have no idea what his name is, but for some reason, that doesn't matter right now.

It's strange writing to you when I don't even know your name, but does it even matter? For me, it's part of the mystery of this situation. In fact, the mystery of this makes my heart race. The care I feel in your words makes me feel things I've never experienced in all of my twenty-five years.

I can't put my finger on
what exactly it is that makes me
want to keep this going,
but I like the idea of knowing
more about you before
I actually meet you. Learning about
the man you are through
your words means more to me than
being able to see your face.
More than knowing your name.

It frightens me more than you can
understand. Partly because
I try to wrap my mind around
falling for someone
without meeting them.
It's like you're pulling me to you,
and I have no control.
I try to wrap my mind around
how this can fit in my life.

I WANT THESE THINGS. I WANT A LIFE,
BUT I ALSO WANT A LIFE FULL
OF LOVE. IT'S CRAZY TO TALK
LIKE THIS, BUT IS THAT POSSIBLE
BETWEEN US?
IT SEEMS LIKE YOU'RE TRYING
TO TAKE OVER MY DOUBT FILLED WORLD
AND MAKE ME A BELIEVER.
THIS SITUATION JUST MIGHT WORK OUT.
TESSA

I hop out of the car and dart across the dark tree-lined street and onto the dimly lit porch. I stick the bright pink sticky notes firmly on the door and quickly make my way back to the car, running the whole way. When I slip back into the driver seat and close the car door, my heart beating against my chest, I inhale deeply. I think I just made my life a little more complicated. Every moment I spend with Lenox and every time I write to this mystery guy, my heart gets a little more involved. And a lot more confused.

November 1, 2015

It's the first day in a little over six months since I last wrote my thoughts down in a journal. It was always an outlet for me to get my feelings out. My dreams. My wants. I stopped writing when I stopped believing in my dreams and wants. I lost this part of me until a girl. A smart, beautiful, and funny girl found my journal. A woman who was searching for the same kind of dreams and wants I've longed for in my life. I've started writing again today because I think maybe I'm ready to open up to the possibility that those desires are still attainable.

Lenox

CHAPTER
26

Lenox

I 'VE READ THE WORDS ON these three pink sticky notes
more times than I can count. I'm trying to piece together what
has changed because something has definitely changed. I play
over the words I wrote to her in the letters up to this point that could
have chipped away at the wall she's built so that I could slip through
it. I've definitely moved through it.

Tessa is more open. She's more willing to accept the possibility
of love. She has softened.

It's everything I've wanted from the start, but an uneasy feeling
is clouding my ability to savor the moment. To be happy, I've
reached her. Maybe it's because I know the real flesh and blood Lenox has had a part in it. When we're together, I can see her walls
coming down. I need to tell her. I want to tell her the two guys vying
for her heart are actually the same person.

I'm not sure she is ready to hear that quite yet and telling her
now may cause her to put that wall back up. It has to be the right
moment. The right time. Just a few more dates. A couple more letters

so I can be sure.

I need to be sure because I fear this time I won't recover.

I'm working in the back of the store when Sam comes in with a shit eating grin on his face. "Dude, there's someone here to see you," he announces. "She is hotter close up than she is from a distance." As usual, I have an overwhelming urge to punch him. I'm assuming he's talking about Tessa, but you never know with Sammy.

"Sam, I'm going to presume you're talking about Tessa. I'm also going to take this moment to give you the benefit of the doubt and believe you will shut your mouth when it comes to her in the future." I make sure he understands my meaning by giving him a poignant look.

"Shit, man, this is serious," he says without apology.

Shaking my head, I walk past him and out into the store. I immediately spot her standing in the new releases. She's reading the back of an album, and she doesn't see me. It allows me time to observe her without her knowing it. I don't think Tessa knows just how beautiful she is, the smoothness of her skin, or the way she takes my breath away when she smiles when no one is watching like she has a secret. She completely takes me.

When I take another step toward her, she turns as if sensing my presence and her grin brightens. It feels so good to know that look is just for me.

"Hey," I say almost breathlessly. "Hey," she says back quietly. "I'm sorry I just stopped by like this, but I was close by and wanted to see you." Her cheeks flush as soon as the words leave her lips.

"Tessa, never apologize. I always want to see you," I reassure her. My response is only deepening the color in her cheeks.

We stand only inches apart in the crowded store watching one another silently. As if she snaps out of trance, Tessa says, "I did stop by for a reason, although I could've texted or called you, I was wondering if you might want to have dinner tomorrow night?"

I can't stop the elation from taking over my face.

"I would love to have dinner tomorrow night. Should I pick you up around seven o'clock?" I reply without hesitation.

"Actually, I was thinking of making dinner for you at my house, but seven o'clock is perfect," she clarifies. "Would that be okay?"

She wants to make me dinner. It's sweet, and the innocent way she is watching makes me fall a little bit more.

"Tessa, that sounds perfect," I assure her. There has been a gradual shift in our relationship, and it's more noticeable every day. I need to find a way to get everything out in the open so we can move forward. Beyond this friendship—this connection. Leaving all of the secrets behind us.

"Okay, great!" She says with a charming enthusiasm. "Uh, well, okay I guess I need to get back to work and so do you."

Leaning in I press my lips to her cheek, not caring who is watching. When I pull back, I look her directly in the eyes. "I'm really glad you stopped by, and I look forward to tomorrow night," I confess to her.

"Me too," she says, quietly. She lifts her hand in a shy wave before turning around and walking away from me. I watch her until she walks through the door and leaves the building.

This girl makes me feel everything I spent so much time trying to avoid having in my life.

When I get home, I decide to respond to Tessa's latest sticky notes.

Tessa,

It feels amazing to know you feel what I am. It's hard to be confident in something unseen. Feelings can be so complicated, and it takes a lot for a person to believe in them. To accept that sometimes these things are completely out of our control.

I want this to work, too. I want to learn about everything that makes up the person you are right now. I want to know the person you hope to be. Things can get so muddled when we let all the outside factors of starting a relationship get in the way. This is our opportunity to do things the way we want to do them. I know it won't be long before I want you to look into my eyes and know everything. I want you to see me and know my name. I want you to know I write these words for you. I want you to feel them in my touch.

This relationship is more than just words between us. It is more than the need to help you and me believe again. You're almost there. I'm almost there, and we can believe together. Until then, please know that no matter what, all of this is true. I think I've said it before, but I need you to understand I mean it. Every word I say to you is true.

Me

November 5, 2015

Every time I'm with Tessa, my feelings get stronger, which only makes keeping this secret harder. I need to tell her. I should tell her. I can see a future unfolding between us, both in the letters and in person. I've got to find the right time to tell her.

CHAPTER 27

TESSA

I READ THE LETTER LEFT on my desk this afternoon for the third time. I analyze everything from the words to the way he phrases his sentences. It's sincere and emotional without revealing too much about himself.

I've been honest with him. I want to discover what this unexplainable pull is between us. I need to understand why I want to know him. No, that's not right. I need to understand why I need to know him.

Resting my head on the palms of my hands, I release a long, drawn out breath.

The only problem is these letters are creating turmoil within me because as much as I'm pulled to the guy writing these letters, I feel an indefinable connection with Lenox. My mind is as confused as my heart. I've never been in this kind of situation.

I'm the girl who can't find a guy to hold my attention. I've never been intrigued to the point my thoughts are consumed by anyone before these letters began appearing in my office. Never have I longed to spend every free moment with a guy because he makes me laugh at the same time he gives me butterflies. Confused. This is exactly what I am right now, and I'm not sure what I should do about it all.

I don't want to hurt anyone, and I don't want to be the one hurt. I'm beginning to trust and have faith that the things I've spent years denying are possible for me.

Dashing down the hallway, I turn the corner to where Chad's office is located. I only have so much time before I have to be out the door so I can have everything done for dinner with Lenox tonight.

I open the door at the same time I knock. He's on the phone when I walk in and signals to me he will be off in a moment and to sit down.

It's always a little strange for me to watch him work. I'm so used to his constant revolving door of shenanigans and less than serious attitude. My lips turn up at the corners as he talks to one of our donors on the phone. He's really pretty brilliant at his job. He balances his professionalism with a sincere personal level of work, which works well with our type of clients. It fills me with an odd sense of pride. Chad has been the one person I could count on for more years than I can count these days. I trust him with my life, which is why I'm here. I need his honest opinion, and if there is one thing I can count on from Chad, it's his honesty.

He gives me his trademark smile as he says his goodbyes before hanging up the phone.

As soon as the receiver is back in its rightful place, he leans forward, his elbows on his desk and his chin resting on his hands. "What's up, Buttercup?"

"Oh, you know. The usual, my love life in shambles," I say, sarcastically.

"Honey, shambles is not the word I would use to describe your love life right now," he states. "A little crowded maybe, but definitely not a disaster."

I know he's right. This isn't my typical problem when it comes to guys. Usually, my issue is the fact I can't find a good one. That is not my problem right now.

"Fine, it's not horrible, but I'm confused and stressed nonetheless," I admit, truthfully.

"Tessa, you have nothing to feel guilty about when it comes to your dilemma."

"I don't feel guilty," I interrupt.

"You've got guilt written all over your face, sweetie," he teases. "The thing is Tessa; your situation is no different than any other dating situation. You have nothing to feel guilty about when it comes to these two guys. My only advice is to stop thinking about what everyone else will think and think only of yourself for once. Think about what and who makes you happy. It's the only thing that matters in the end."

"What if I don't know?" I ask him sincerely.

"You will, but I do want to point out once again that you have one in flesh and blood and the other you've never spent any real time with. I think the question is really going to be how long can you keep doing this when you don't really know what you're dealing with. I say while you can, take your time, and listen to your heart for once."

Chad leans forward placing a kiss on my forehead.

"I love you, Buttercup," he tells me, softly. It's a rare moment when Chad lets his feelings be so exposed without sarcasm.

Standing up, I kiss his cheek before turning to the door. "I love you, too."

I may not know what I'm doing about the quandary I'm currently in, but I feel better about how to handle myself.

Before I leave my office, I decide to respond to the letter as quickly as I can so I have time to drop them off before heading home.

I lay the pad out on my desk and pick up my pen. I just need, to be honest and open about how I feel then we can figure things out as we go along.

Hi. When I got your letter today, I read it several times. I think your honesty and forthcoming comments left me feeling more involved and more confused. I'm not very good at being out of control, especially when it come to my emotions, but I'm working on it. I'll try to keep looking forward. I want, to be honest, though. This makes me nervous. I worry about getting hurt. I worry about hurting you. You started something that I can't seem to stop. It made me open to not only you but other things and people in my life. I guess I should thank you for it, but I also hope I don't regret it. You want me to be honest, and I want, to be honest. I'm still scared, but I'm starting to understand why people fall in love. And I owe it all to you.

I hope you know my words are true, too. When I get your letters, everything else disappears, but then I realize my life goes on after these letters. I'm honest, but how do I keep all that I'm feeling together. It's something I want to figure out, together. Until next time.

Tessa

November 8, 2015

The days are getting better and better. My feelings for Tessa are blooming into something I've never felt. Something I want. Everything I need.

CHAPTER
28

Lenox

I T'S A FEW MINUTES BEFORE seven when I arrive at Tessa's door. I stand there staring at the door, thinking about my last letter to her and the sticky note I found on my door when I got home from work today. It's strange to think she is unaware it's me writing to her, and sometimes it bothers me to know she must think she's involved with two different people. Yet, I realize that's unfair because we've made no commitments. The ironic thing is I feel positive that both relationships are having a direct impact on the other.

I feel her opening more when I'm with her and also in her words. The time is coming, I'll tell her, but tonight I'm going to enjoy just being with her.

Raising my fist, I rap three quick knocks on the door.

I hear movement on the other side of the door. Her muted voice lets me know she will be right here. The door swings open. My mouth nearly falls open. Tessa is standing before me, smiling. She looks beautiful. She has on very little makeup. Her cheeks are a rosy color, and her lips have a light pink gloss to them that make them appear full. The spaghetti strapped floral dress hits just above her knees, flowing slightly at her small hips. My eyes travel down her shapely legs to her bare feet. Seeing her bare feet does something to me. She looks relaxed. It's breathtaking.

"Hello." Her voice sounds breathy. When I look back up to her face, the color in her cheeks has deepened letting me know she's aware of my lingering gaze. "Hi," I manage to get out. She smiles timidly.

Opening the door wider, she invites me in. "Please come in, dinner is almost ready. Would you like some wine or a beer maybe?" I can't take my eyes off of her. She has her back to me, and as she walks, there is a slight sway to her hips. My awareness of her is in overdrive tonight. I follow her into the kitchen. "A glass of wine would be great."

Tessa walks over to the cabinet; her back is still to me. She rises up on her tip toes to reach the wine glass on the top shelf; her dress lifts a little higher revealing more skin. My legs move at their own volition toward her. Placing my hands on her waist, I hold her steady. Her breath catches, and I feel a shiver run through her body. Leaning forward, I place a kiss on her cheek.

This is the first time since the night I put her to bed I've been this close to her. The smell of lilac is clouding my mind, hypnotizing me.

Turning in my grasp, Tessa faces me. Our gazes lock, neither of us says a word. We only look into one another's eyes. I reach up and brush an errant strand of hair that has fallen into her eyes. "Lenox," she breathes my name, sending a warm sensation to the pit of my stomach. There is something different about the way she says my name.

My eyes drop to her shiny lips when she bites the bottom one and pulls it between her teeth.

Swallowing the knot that has formed in my throat, I sigh, "Tessa." I say her name, worshiping every syllable. Slowly, I lean toward her until our lips meet, my eyes never leaving hers. A tiny moan slips between our lips as I deepen the kiss, and her arms wrap around my neck.

All my senses have been ignited; I can feel her, smell her, and see every emotion the simple touch of our lips creates within us.

My hands run up her back, and I pull her closer to me just about the time the oven timer rings through the kitchen, stopping us. I want to beg her not to stop.

Her voice full of regret, she whispers, "The food is ready."

Reluctantly, I release her, and she unwraps her arms from around my neck.

"Let's eat because I'm already ready for dessert," I say, teasingly.

A wide grin brightens her face, and she slaps me on the arm as she moves around me to the oven.

"You sit down, and if you eat all of your dinner then you'll get dessert," she teases.

As I leave the room, I glance back at her and realize that this shift between us is everything I've wanted.

After dinner we clear the table together, then both make ourselves comfortable on the couch. I'm not sure how long we sit here chatting and laughing at one another. She teases me after I tell her that I haven't been able to stop thinking about the book I read the night I stayed on her couch.

The atmosphere of the room suddenly changes when she runs her fingers through my hair and over my cheek. "You trimmed your beard. I like it," she tells me. She's looking at me; her gaze is heated, and the fire inside me is suddenly ignited once again.

Reaching my hand out, I cup her cheek, and she leans into it. "Do you know what you do to me?"

Shaking her head, she quietly stands up and takes my hand in hers, gently tugging until I stand up. She begins leading me down the hallway to her room. A voice in my head whispers, tell her, but my heart says it's not the time. I've fallen for this girl, and she wants me. I want her too.

When we enter her bedroom, she pulls me toward her bed then turns around. Standing in front of me, I can see it on her face she's nervous, but she's trusting me. Knowing her, I realize her trust isn't something she gives away easily. A timid smile forms on her face, and she gives me a small nod, answering the question I asked her with my eyes.

Gradually, I lift my hand to her shoulder, taking the strap of her dress in my fingertips and sliding it off her shoulder. She turns, giving me access to the zipper running down her back then turns back to me. The other strap falls, and the dress slips down, pooling at her feet.

I step back a little, taking in the way she looks standing before me. Her peach colored skin feels smooth to my touch; a gasp escapes her lips when my hand comes back to rest on her waist. Her eyes are closed, so I say "Tessa, open your eyes and look at me." She does as I ask and the desire I see in the depths tell me what I need to know, but I need to ask anyway. "Are you sure you want this with me? If not, tell me now because the further we go, the harder it will be for us to stop."

"Lenox, I want you. I've never been surer about anything in my life," she vows. Tessa makes the first move and reaches her hands out, taking my shirt by the hem. Lifting it over my head, I finish taking it off. She runs her hands down my chest, sending a shiver through me. Her hands move to the button of my jeans, but I stop her.

"Let's take this slow," I tell her, my voice barely above a whisper. She just nods as I lean forward placing kisses over her shoulders, up her neck over to her soft lips. Once our lips touch, it takes everything in me to keep things slow. I can tell she is fighting it, too.

Then she bites my lip, and I lose all sense. I bite her back. This sends us both over the edge, and the remainder of our clothes are off before I can even think clearly. My lips caress every inch of her body. I'm not sure how it happens, but before I know it she is pushing me down on the bed and slowly crawling over me. Leaving her mark with her lips along the way up until she claims my mouth once again. Tessa takes control, and I gladly let her.

My entire body is willing to be her puppet. She owns me.

We continue our assault on one another's senses until neither of us can take it another second. "Lenox, I want you," she moans. This is all I need to hear.

Flipping her over, I take the control back. I give her one last hard kiss then I reach for my jeans and my wallet. Pulling out a condom, I thank God I listened in sex ed and always learned to be prepared.

Tessa watches me as I kneel over her. The heat in her eyes is burning bright. Once I'm ready, I position myself over her and look directly into her eyes. Whispering, I tell her, "Tessa, I want you, too," as I swiftly enter her.

She moans my name and the world around us disappears. It's just me, Tessa and this overwhelming feeling of love for her.

Tessa and I didn't leave her bed the rest of the night. We wrapped ourselves around one another, telling stories and sharing ourselves. I shared everything but the fact I've been writing her letters for the past few months. It wasn't the right moment to divulge that truth, but it is time.

I realized the moment she completely gave herself to me that we are meant to be, and we can only work with my total honesty.

As we snuggled through the morning, I concocted a plan. We're having dinner tonight; I mapped out every detail of the night in my mind while I watched her sleeping in my arms.

Now as I drive home, I feel confident tonight will end with both Tessa and me wondering why we ever doubted the existence of love and romance again.

Just as the thought crosses my mind, I'm turning into my driveway and spot someone sitting on my porch. At first, I think it's my mom, but I can't figure out why she didn't use her key to go in. When I pull to a stop, I quickly hop out and dash toward the porch, "Mom, …"

My voice catches in my throat, and I stop dead in my tracks. It's not my mom waiting for me.

"Sara?" My voice comes out harsher than intended, but my mind can't wrap around the fact she is standing here, in front of me.

She's everything I remember, from her smile to the way her hair hangs long over her shoulder.

"Hello, Lenox," She says in a sweet, low voice.

Snapping back to reality, I greet her again, "Hello, Sara. What are you doing here?" She flinches at my question. "I'm back in town visiting my parents, and I wanted to stop by." I can tell she wants to continue but is holding back. She's debating if she should say what she really came here to say.

"I don't understand why you think it's alright just to show up on my doorstep," I spat, not caring if I hurt her feelings. She has the nerve to show up, and it has to be when I've finally moved past us and our relationship.

Wringing her hands together, she looks nervously around her. "Lenox, I didn't come here to fight. I just wanted to see how you are and apologize for the way I ended things."

"You just left me. You had no regard for the ten years I loved you. You left with a single note of goodbye and no real explanation. Now you want to see how I am?"

"Lenox, I know I don't deserve your forgiveness, but I want you to know I was wrong. I'm not asking you to take me back. I just want you to know that I should have been honest. If we had been honest about everything between us, if I had told you about my doubts, then maybe things could've been different. I should've trusted you."

I push past Sara, wanting to get away from her.

"Damn right, Sara! You should have trusted me, but instead, you ruined everything. You ruined our relationship and our friendship." I laugh, and it sounds so out of place. When I look at her now, I don't feel the heartache she left me with anymore. "It doesn't matter anymore. I don't hate you anymore; I don't even think about you. In fact, you probably did me a favor because I was so blind. I'm not trying to get back at you by saying these things; for hurting me. What we had was good and taught me so much. It led me to who I am to-day, so thank you for that."

"Wow," she huffs. "I'm actually glad to hear you say all of this to me. I said what I need to; I just needed you to know I'm sorry, and I hope you will be happy in your life."

Without another word, Sara turns and walks away from me. There is no sadness. No anger. The only thing on my mind is the fact I know I can have a happy life now, and it's all because of Tessa.

November 11, 2015

I'm happy. It's been a long time since I felt this way. I never dreamed I could move past the heartache of losing Sara, but I have and I did. Now, I just need to trust this happiness. I need to think about what Tessa makes me feel, but also what she does to prove I can trust her. The biggest thing is she is trusting me. It's time.

CHAPTER 29

TESSA

WHEN THE POUNDING ON MY door starts, I rush over to answer it. I know it's Chad because he told me he would be here in no more than twenty minutes when I called him after Lenox left. Pulling the door open, I barely have it all the way open before Chad is rushing past me.

"Details! I need details," he exclaims as he turns to face me, handing me a muffin and latte in the process. "I thought you might need sustenance after such an eventful night."

While I appreciate the muffin and latte, I object to his assumptions about my night. "Seriously, you're ridiculous! I'm hungry, but it has nothing to do with my night."

Waving his hand in the air dismissing my statement, Chad makes himself comfortable on the couch. "Okay, Buttercup, spill it. You can't just call me, tell me Lenox stayed the night, and then expect not to divulge some details."

"Lenox stayed the night," I state simply, trying to sound nonchalant about it when everything in me is still floating on cloud nine.

Chad's mouth falls open. "I may never get used to you sounding so blasé about all of this. A guy stayed the night at your house, in your bed, and you seem so calm about it," he proclaims. "What does this mean? It means something because you would never let this happen if it didn't mean something big."

I want to laugh at the fact I have shocked and confused the ever calm and together, Chad Borchgardt. I can't help smiling because honestly, I've never felt happier than I do at this very moment. Well, except maybe last night with Lenox and possibly this morning before he left. Yep, pretty much every moment I've spent with him.

A loud gasp echoes through the room. "Oh my God! You're in love with him!"

"What?" I try to sound like he is completely wrong, but instead, I nearly choke on the word.

"You, Tessa Marie Collins are in love with one, Lenox Malone," Chad declares. "I've never been so excited or proud in my entire life. You finally have what I know you deserve. I've seen it before today, but I didn't want to say anything until I was sure. And, I'm very sure because it is written all over your face."

My heart feels like it may beat right out of my chest. I'm in love. I don't deny it. Instead, I look at Chad and start laughing and crying. I'm laughing and crying so hard; I suddenly hear Chad join in, and he pulls me into a hug.

"Oh my God, I love him. This is terrible," I say through my tears. Shaking his head, Chad says, "No, it's not. Tessa, it's wonderful."

"But, what if I get hurt. What if he doesn't love me back?" My fears begin to take over my mind, and now my tears are made of something different.

"Sweetie, I think you already know how he feels for you. Think about it," Chad insists, gently.

I think back to the night before and every moment between Lenox and me that led us to last night. He did ask me to dinner tonight because he said he had something he wanted to tell me.

Looking up at Chad, I smile. "Yeah, I think I do."

As Chad pulls me into another hug, a tiny ache begins to build in my chest. I've fallen for Lenox, but a part of me feels like I might be missing something.

———

I've moved through my day feeling like a new person. The way I feel is so different than anything I imagined. I, Tessa Collins am undeniably in love. It's a miracle, I think and laugh out loud as I walk down the street.

I stop by my office to grab some papers I need to review before Monday, and since I'm close, I decide to run into the coffee shop for a latte. I plan on spending the rest of the day relaxing until my dinner date with Lenox tonight.

When I enter the shop, I notice it's unusually crowded. Glancing around I take in the differences between the weekday crowd and to-day. As my eyes roam over the room, they lock on one individual I wasn't expecting to see. My heart rate speeds up at the sight of him. Lenox. I watch him; he doesn't see me yet. He appears to be writing in something. He looks content; it's nice to see him looking as happy as I am.

Winding my way through the crowd and around tables, I walk up to him, "Hi," I say, shyly.

I hate to interrupt him, but I couldn't pretend not to see him.

He glances up at me, and I can tell I startled him a little. "Tessa," he says my name, looking surprised yet happy to see me. He closes the book he was writing in and pushes it to the side.

"What are you doing here?"

Shrugging my shoulders, I reply, "I had to run into the office and decided I wanted to get a drink."

Standing up, he leans in and places a kiss softly to my lips. "Well, I'm glad you did. How are you?" He pulls a chair out for me to take a seat. "I'm good," I tell him as I sit down.

He takes his seat again. His hand reaches for mine. Lenox begins to stroke my hand as he looks at me. It brings to mind my conversation with Chad this morning. *Sweetie, I think you already know how he feels for you. Think about it.* Chad told me, and I think he's right if the way Lenox is looking at me is any indication.

"Are you still up for tonight?" Nodding, I answer him at the same time. "Absolutely, I wouldn't miss it."

"Good," he says smiling. "I've got so much to tell you...to say."

"You're driving me nuts. Tell me now," I whine, laughing.

He looks so serious when he says, "No, not yet. It's not the right time."

"Fine, you win," I concede. I reach my hand up to push his hair back, unable to resist not touching him.

"Did you order, yet?" he asks as if it's natural for us to be together.

"Nope, I saw you before I made it to the line," I answer. I forgot all about my latte the moment I saw Lenox. "I'll get it for you. Wait here," he tells me as he stands up, placing another kiss to my lips as he slips past me.

I watch him as he moves around the crowd. It's a little reminiscent of the first time we came here together. I watched him from afar, wondering why I felt like this guy was about to change my life and I was meant to find him. I almost laugh remembering how he told me I would one day be thinking back on our date, and now I'm doing exactly that, he was right. So annoying I think as I laugh to myself, a smirk on my face while my eyes never leave Lenox.

He looks over at me at just about the same time and gives me a questioning look, like what's that look for?

If he only knew, my God, I'm becoming the kind of girl I envied my whole life. The one who has everything together with someone she loves by her side.

People continue to pour in and out of the coffee shop, Lenox is slowly but surely moving up in the line, giving me a sweet grin every once in a while.

He's finally ordering when suddenly two teenage boys are messing around and bump into the table, sending Lenox's notebook flying off the table. They apologize as they walk away, I wave them off because I feel so good they could have knocked my whole cup of coffee on me, and I probably wouldn't care.

I reach down to pick up Lenox's book and notice a folded sheet of paper has slipped out and under the table next to us, so I get on my knees and reach for it, grabbing a hold of it and pulling it safely out. Standing back up and sitting down again, I go to stick the paper back into his book.

Suddenly, I freeze as my eyes fix on my name scribbled on the outside of the folded sheet of paper. It isn't my name that has me instantly feeling extremely nauseous. It's the handwriting, but this doesn't make sense. Except I would know that handwriting anywhere. Why does Lenox have it?

I unfold it slowly, my nausea intensifying with each fold. Once I have it unfolded, my eyes scan the words written inside.

Tessa,

How do I tell you what I should have told you months ago? How do I explain to you why I've kept this secret from you? You've probably guessed it the moment you saw my handwriting, but I, Lenox Malone, am the same guy who has been writing you for the last several months. It's my journal you found. It's my words you've been reading, and it's my mind you've changed. Tessa, I've fallen...

Abruptly, I stand up and drop the letter. It floats slowly to the ground. "Tessa?" I hear Lenox say my name, but I'm stunned speechless.

My shaking hand moves over my mouth quickly because I'm afraid I'm going to scream, or I'm going to be sick. I feel a hand on my arm; I can't even shake it off. My gaze lifts and locks on a set of familiar eyes.

I see the moment he knows I know, and I begin shaking my

head side to side.

Desperately, he grips my arms. "Let me explain!" I pull away as hard as I can, and he reluctantly releases me. "Tessa, please...just," he begs, rubbing his hand down his bearded face. "Please," he says in barely a whisper.

Backing away, I shake my head. "Why did you do this? You weren't supposed to hurt me. You said, to be honest," I ramble. A sob escapes my lips, and I know I need to get out of here. "Tessa, please..." Cutting him off, I shout, "No!" Everyone else around us is non-existent.

Crying, I say one last thing to him before I turn and leave. "My God, Lenox. I fell in love with you."

I don't remember leaving or how I got to Chad's, but I do remember the look in Lenox's eyes when I told him I fell in love with him. Even more, I'll never forget what it's like to have my heart break in two.

November 12, 2015

She knows and I didn't get to tell her. I screwed up. How do I fix this? I need to figure out how I can fix this. She feels betrayed. Tessa said I made her look like a fool, but the reality is, I'm the fool. I didn't trust her when she was the one person I should have trusted. My fear broke her heart. I. Broke. Her.

Heart. I broke my heart.

CHAPTER 30

Lenox

I T'S BEEN THREE DAYS. THREE days since Tessa told me she fell in love with me then turned and walked away. I thought my heart shattered when Sara left, but nothing compares to the torment I felt watching her leave and knowing I had no one to blame but myself.

Three days and two bottles of tequila. Drinking away my pain only lasts so long. It doesn't really help, so I'm not sure why I keep doing it. I guess it's because I'm numb for a while until I pass out. I haven't showered, and I've barely eaten. Even Roosevelt won't come near me.

Curled up on the couch, I bury myself further into the blankets surrounding me.

I'm going to get up eventually, but later. I'll get up later when everything stops hurting. Just when I think my head can't hurt any worse, a loud bang echoes through my living room.

"Nox, this is bullshit! Get your ass up!" Sammy's voice rattles what's left of my brain. Maybe if I don't move then, he won't see me. "God damn it, Nox, where the fuck are you? You aren't doing this again. Your mom is on her way over here, and you aren't going to let her see you like this again. I broke eighteen different traffic laws trying to beat her here."

Just before he yanks the covers off of me, I feel him standing there. I don't have time to move.

"Sam, get the fuck off of me," I scream just before water hits me in the face. I fly off the couch, swinging, but I don't hit anything but air. "I'm going to kill you."

"Dude, get your shit together and take a shower," he sounds serious, something I'm not used to from Sammy. "Like I said, your mom will be here any minute. I'll start cleaning up around here, but I won't let you put her through this again."

I look at him through my bloodshot eyes. He is watching me with concern and a sort of pity. It pisses me off. "I'll take a shower, but don't ever fucking look at me like you feel sorry for me again."

Slowly, I walk out of the living room and down the hall to take a shower. I wish I thought this might help, but for once I agree with Sam. My mom can't see me this way. This is worse than Sara and it nearly broke her to watch me in so much pain. I tried to push her away. I tried to protect my mom from my pain then, and she wouldn't allow it. In her words, if I hurt then she hurts.

And, damn it I'm hurting so fucking bad.

I may have taken the longest shower of my life. I tried washing away the stink and sorrow of three days, hoping the pain would go with it. It didn't work.

As I got dressed, I could hear my mom and Sammy whispering in the living room, but I couldn't make out what they were saying to one another. It doesn't even matter. I know what they are trying to do. They're going to try and fix this, and as much I wish they could; they can't. I screwed up.

Making my way down the hall and into the living room, I walk directly into the kitchen, filling up a glass of water and downing it in one gulp. I don't even look at them, but I can feel them silently watching me from the living room over the bar.

My mom moves first and walks around the counter, approaching me cautiously like she doesn't know what I might do. Timidly, she places her hand on my shoulder, but I still don't look at her. I'm not sure if I can hold it together if I do. She takes a deep breath then sighs my name, "Lenox. What happened?"

Looking over at her, I take her hand from my shoulder and hold it mine. "Mom, I screwed up. You told me. Hell, even Sammy told me," I say, raising my hand in the direction Sammy is still quietly standing. "You both told me, to be honest with her." "Oh, Lenox, you…" she starts to say, but I interrupt her.

"This is on me, Mom. This pain I'm feeling is my fault. I asked her over and over to trust me, but I was too scared to trust her." I laugh even though nothing about what I'm feeling or saying is funny. "I was so scared Tessa might break my heart that I held back one important piece of our relationship. The most important piece. I betrayed her and in turn, I broke not only her heart but mine, too."

I push away from the counter, dropping her hand and walking into the living room.

"Dude, have you explained to her?" Sam asks me. Even through my fog of self-loathing, I can appreciate his concern.

"Yes, maybe if you just explain to her," my mom chimes in.

Whipping around to face them, I shake my head. "Don't you see? What is there to explain? I asked her to believe in me, and I couldn't even give her the truth." I put my face in my hands, and a few tears fall. "I never thought it possible, but this is a thousand times worse than Sara because I had control in preventing this heartache for both of us. It hurts more because I know Tessa is hurting, too. I saw her heart break when I looked in her eyes."

My mom comes to my side and wraps her arms around me.

"You listen to me, Lenox Michael Malone, do you really love

this girl?" I look up at her like she's crazy. Hasn't she been listening to me the last ten minutes? "If you love this girl then you find a way to help her understand. Does she love you?" I let her words sink in. "Lenox, does she love you?" she asks me again.

Nodding my head, I answer her, "She told me she fell in love with me right before she walked away,"

My mom placed her hand on her mouth, and her shoulders sagged for a moment then she straightened. "You help her understand, Lenox."

"But, how?" I ask desperately.

Hugging me again, she says, "Oh, honey, only you know how to do that, but I'm confident you know what will reach her heart. You've done it once so you can do it again."

My heart still aches, but I feel something else. A little something else, but it's there. It's hope.

Sammy and my mom stayed for a while, trying to cheer me up and giving ideas on what might win Tessa's heart back. Of course, neither of them realized that I already knew what I needed to do.

My mom was right when she said I reached her heart once, and I could do it again. Damn, I hope she hasn't put that wall completely up again. I pull out a sheet of paper and begin pouring my heart out. This time as someone in love. As someone who believes that there is the love he is meant to have, not only that he is meant to have, but that is meant to have him.

I'm just going to have to romance Tessa again with my words.

November 15, 2015

It's been seven days. One week since I've seen or heard from Tessa. The pain I feel now compares nothing to what I've felt in the past. She's destroyed me. No. No, I'm wrong. I did this to myself. I destroyed me.

CHAPTER 31

TESSA

I TAKE A SIP OF the hot cup of coffee my mom just poured for me. She sits across their kitchen table from me silently, waiting for me to start talking. We've been sitting here for twenty minutes, and I haven't said a word. I walked into my parents' house, saw my mom, and began sobbing.

As soon as she figured out I wasn't physically injured, she began trying to coax why I was a miserable mess out of me to no avail. I couldn't speak. She caught on that no amount of consoling was going to get me to talk at that moment, so she quietly held me. When the crying slowed, she led me into the kitchen, sat me down, and then proceeded to move around the kitchen. She made coffee and pulled out cookies before taking a seat directly in front of me without speaking. Just waiting. Waiting for me to be ready to open up to her.

She's always had this unbelievable patience with me.

The sobbing has stopped and now only a runaway tear escapes my eyes, wiping the latest one away, I look up at her.

Reaching her hand across the table, she takes mine in hers. "Are you ready to tell me what's going on with you?" It's just like her, never pushing me, always giving me a choice.

"Mo, was falling in love with Dad easy for you?" I wipe another errant tear away.

The shock of my question is evident on my mother's face. I've never asked her a question like this before; we've never discussed falling in love. Just as quickly as it appears, it's gone.

Squeezing my hand, she sighs, "Tessa, falling in love isn't the hard part, it's accepting it." More tears begin to fall quietly down my cheeks. "Honey, have you fallen in love?" She isn't asking in her usual meddling way.

"Oh, Mo, I think I've fallen so hard for him, and the situation is so complicated," I huff out. "I've spent years avoiding this very complication. I've always been so scared of getting hurt. Frightened I would never find what you and Daddy have together."

"Tessa, there's always a risk, but you'll never know if it's lasting if you don't give it a chance," she shares with me. "You need to ask yourself, do you feel more pain at the thought of living without him or with him?"

I let her words sink in. Can I imagine my life moving forward without Lenox? Can I live without his humor and kindness? Can I live without his words or his gentle touch?

While I think about what she's saying, she continues, "Never compare your love with what your father and I have, Tessa. It's our meant to be. Everyone's meant to be is different. You have your own, and the only thing you need to do is recognize and never let it go. That is the scary part, the idea you might let something great pass you by. Don't let the unknown possibilities hold you back because it works both ways. There's the possibility to have an incredible love and life."

Her words sink in, and I realize she's right. I have so much to think about where Lenox is concerned. He kept a big truth from me. It hurt, but is it unforgivable?

Standing up, I walk around the table to my mother's side. She stands up and pulls me into her comforting embrace. As she strokes my hair, I again find myself crying. "Tessa, I know I don't have all of the details where this young man is concerned, but if he earned your love at all, then he must be something special. Just let yourself be happy.

I spend most of the night thinking about what Mo said and what it means for Lenox and me. I've definitely fallen in love with him. I just don't know if I trust myself or him.

When I think about the fact that he kept it a secret that he was the guy writing me those letters and he knew the whole time, I feel like a fool. Does he even realize how I struggled and was tormented by thoughts that I was betraying him, both the guy in the letters and the guy I spent my time with for the last few months?

Now I need to find a way to move past this, past the embarrassment of feeling caught between two amazing guys who were actually one in the same. Ugh. Just thinking about it makes it sounds awful.

The biggest question is if once I do move past it, will it be with Lenox or without?

Luckily, my day has been filled with meeting after meeting. It was only at lunch time that I found myself on the verge of crying, so I cut my break short and started helping out the interview crew with processing people into the system.

There were several times that Chad tried to bring up Lenox, and I quickly gave him a look to let him know I didn't want to talk. Thank God he got the hint and left it alone. I've let Lenox consume my life enough over the last week. I need all the distractions I can get so I can think about what I want later with a clear mind.

Just when I think I'll make it through the day without having to talk about everything going on, Chad corners me.

"Buttercup, look at me," I turn around and face my best friend, begging him with my eyes to let this go. "I have something to say, and you're going to listen. As your best friend, I can't let you avoid this situation. You can pretend all you want, but it isn't going away. I'll give you some time, but while you're thinking about what you should do, I want to make sure you are thinking about the whole picture."

He stops talking, and the look on his face is telling me he's waiting for me to approve his interference. I know Chad well enough to know he will never let this go unless he can say his piece.

"Fine," I say a little more sharply than I intend.

"I know you're upset. I know you feel betrayed, and you think he lied to you," he begins. I want to correct him when he says to think, but instead, I decide to listen. "I want you to think about every moment you spent with Lenox, and then I want you to think about every word he wrote to you in those letters. You need to think about the things he has told you and the things he revealed so you can see this situation through his eyes. I'm sure he had his reasons and if you love him like I think you do then he deserves for you to consider his feelings in all of this mess, too."

I really hate Chad sometimes. I hate him for his wisdom. I hate him for his interference and his completely annoying way of always being right. He sees me and until Lenox; he may be the only one who has ever truly understood the way I work.

Suddenly, I'm throwing my arms around his neck. "Thank you for understanding me," I whisper.

"I love you, Buttercup, and you deserve to be happy. I won't let anyone ruin that, especially you."

November 25, 2015

Tomorrow is Thanksgiving. I'm thankful to have been given this second chance at love. I'm thankful for fate. I'm thankful for the love and my incapacity for giving up on it. I'm going to get Tessa back, and when I do, I'll show her every day how thankful I am for her love.

CHAPTER 32

Lenox

"WHAT ARE YOU DOING HERE?" Her voice sounds different. Colder. I flinch at the indifference.

I've been waiting outside her door for hours. Determined to see her, I've sat leaning against the wall in the hallway of her building. Waiting. Trying to think of what I would say to her to convince her to hear me out. To take my letter.

Shoving my hands into the pockets of my jeans, it takes everything I have not to reach out to her. Her hair is down, falling over her shoulders in waves. She only has on a light pink lip gloss, making her full lips all the more enticing. A memory of her soft full lips pressed to mine makes my heart feel like it's trying to beat its way out of my chest.

"Lenox, why are you here?" She asks me again, her tone a little less harsh. I'm hurting her. The longer I stand here, staring at her, I can see what my presence is doing. This is as hard for her as it is for me. I've never wanted to hurt Tessa.

I stutter out the words, searching for the right ones. "I…I'm sorry. I had to see you," I croak, tears threatening to fall. She's about to say something I'm sure I don't want to hear, and she really doesn't mean. So I continue, not giving her a chance to speak. "I only came to give you this letter."

"I don't want it," she protests, yet it lacks the force she intended.

"Tessa, please, take it. Read it," I beg, my hands involuntarily reaching out to her.

Backing away, she quickly moves out of my reach. "Don't," she exclaims, her voice shaking. I can see the tears glistening on the edge of her eyelids, waiting to fall.

My arms fall to my sides immediately.

"I'm sorry, just please take this letter and read it," I say desperately. "I only want a chance to explain, and then you can do whatever you want to do with it. Don't be afraid. Don't let fear keep you from believing in what has been happening between us. Just read the letter, Tessa."

Turning her head away from me, Tessa holds out her hand palm up.

It takes me a moment to understand what she's doing. She's going to take the letter. I feel a small flame of hope flicker.

Pulling the letter from my back pocket, I gently place it in her hand, purposefully touching my fingertips to the soft skin of her hands. She tenses as if it hurts her to be this near me.

I turn and walk away. When I reach the end of the hall, I say one last thing without turning back. "I never meant to hurt you."

Before I can walk away, I hear her suck in a breath and the door slamming closed echoes through the hallway.

When I walk through my front door, my Mom is standing in my kitchen, prepping for Thanksgiving dinner tomorrow.

She looks up when the door closes and freezes.

I guess the look on my face tells her everything she needs to know because she rushes around the bar over to me. Throwing her arms around me, she pulls me into her motherly embrace.

"Oh, honey," she says in a soothing voice.

Swallowing the knot that's been lodged in my throat, I barely get out the words. "Mom, I messed up. I've messed things up so bad, and I'm not sure she'll forgive me. I think I'm going to lose her for good."

Rubbing her hand in circles over my back, she continues to hug me. "Lenox, let me ask you something." My mom pushes back out of our embrace. She looks me directly in my eyes. "Did you write to her from the heart?

Nodding my head, I answer her. She asks me another question. "Were you honest? Did you show her you trust her?"

"Yes, yes to all of your questions. That isn't the problem, Mom. The problem is I'm not even sure she will read it and if she doesn't read it then…"

My mother interrupts me, "She'll read it."

"But," I begin to say.

Shaking her head, she takes me by the hand and walks me into the kitchen. "Nope, she'll read it, and the rest is up to her. You've done what you could, honey. Now you trust her and wait."

Now I trust Tessa and wait.

November 26, 2015

It's Thanksgiving. As usual, it'll be mom and me. Tessa will be on my mind. Has she read my letter? I can only wait. There is nothing else for me to do except keep loving her. I'll keep hoping she will forgive me.

TESSA

Tessa,

Forgive me. I would be on my knees begging now if I thought it would work. Instead, I only have what originally brought us together in the first place, my words. My feelings. My vulnerability.

Here it is, all laid out bare for you to do with what you will.

When this started, I didn't want to believe. I didn't want to feel. I didn't want to trust. You changed so much of this for me. From the moment, I read that pink sticky note I fell completely under your spell. I wasn't in control of my emotions. At first, it was just the fact you brought up things I had buried deep inside. Gradually, it became more. I felt this spark. This pull through our exchanges and I couldn't stop. I wanted to stop. God, I wanted to stop so damn bad because I could feel what you were doing to me. I recognized the flame being ignited inside me. It scared the shit out of me.

I looked for you because I didn't have a choice. It was out of my power. It was something greater than me. Bigger than the both of us.

There were so many times I was going to tell you. To let you know. The first moment I saw you, I thought about walking up to you then, but you said you didn't believe in love or romance. The heart I didn't even know I still had cracked a little that day. Sure I could have just walked up to you and took a chance. But, I couldn't. I couldn't allow myself to be vulnerable to anyone. To you.

I realized the only way you might listen. The only way I might be able to convince you was to write you letters. The more I wrote, the bigger this all became. The more it all began to mean. I was sharing my whole self with you through those letters. I was sharing the Lenox you met that day outside of your work when I was with you. Both were, no are the real me. I was just too scared to let you know both sides at the same time. What if you didn't want both. What if it wouldn't last? What if I was wrong and it wasn't real? There were so many what if's and it scared the shit out of me. I was broken once, and I knew I wouldn't survive again.

I wanted you to give me your trust and the ironic thing is I didn't trust you. I wasn't willing to take the chance I so desperately wanted you to take. Then everything changed, you gave me the most precious thing a woman could give a man. You. I knew you trusted me, and I realized I needed to trust you. Stupidly, I thought it needed to be right and perfect when I told you because I still wasn't sure how you would react to finding out my secret, I wanted to have a plan. It doesn't matter now, but I was going to tell you that night at dinner.

Tessa, I realized I should trust you. I wanted to give my heart to you.

I don't know how or when, but somewhere in between losing myself and finding myself again, I fell in love with you. I could be wrong, but you fell in love with me, too.

So, forgive me. Love me. Take a chance on our love. On the romance. On our dreams coming true because Tessa it does exist. I'm still not sure it exists for everyone, but it does exist for us.

Will you take this chance? Find a way to let me know.

Always and Forever,
Lenox

EPILOGUE

TESSA

S TRETCHING MY ARMS OVER MY head, I yawn as I sit up in bed. It was a long sleepless night, and it won't be my last for the foreseeable future. I bury myself back into the soft, fluffy comforter and pull it up to my chin. Maybe I'll stay here just a little longer.

Just when I think it might be possible, my phone rings from the bedside table.

Ugh. No. Go away, I think to myself.

The ringing doesn't stop so I reach over, pick up my phone, and answer it as I pull it to my ear.

"This better be good, or you're in trouble," I scold into the phone.

"Look here Buttercup, I just called to see if you've forgiven him yet?" Chad has never been able to mind his own business.

"None of your business," I hiss softly into the phone. "Is this the only reason you're calling me so early?"

"Honey, I'm supposed to be coming over for dinner tonight. I need to know if I need to arm myself before I enter the second civil war," he insists like he really needs to worry.

"Chad, I'm hanging up now. See you at seven," I inform him before ending the call.

I can hear him still saying something as I press the end call button.

Forgive him? Is he kidding me? Lenox will have to do a lot more if he expects me to forgive him. I'm not giving in. Nope. I won't do it. He can't sweet talk me or flash me that dimpled smile. It's going to take more than a simple I'm sorry. He hurt my feelings, and I deserve more.

Okay, I'm going to get up, go about my day as I normally would, and hope I can survive the day on a few hours sleep.

Releasing a long drawn out sigh as I push the covers back, I sit up quickly, placing my feet on the floor. Lifting my gaze, I see an envelope taped to the table next to me.

It never fails, an envelope has the power to send my heart racing, never mind what's inside of it.

Lenox

Tessa,

I guess I'll never make the perfect choices or decisions. Sometimes I'll get it all wrong. You should know that better than anyone. I can only tell you I'm sorry and hope you forgive me. I didn't mean to hurt you. Truly, I didn't mean to forget my promise. I should have come out and told you. I know you hate secrets. I know you hate half-truths. But, I love you. Everything I do is for you. For our life. For our future. You are my dream. Every day. Every moment has led me to loving you. I'm sorry I was late. Forgive me. Look up now and forgive me.

Always and forever,

Lenox

I peer through the crack of the doorway, watching as a tear slips down her face. She looks up, and I can see it in her eyes. She's going to forgive me like she always does. Looking down, I gaze into the curious blue eyes that match his mothers and give him a thumbs up.

"She forgives me, buddy," I whisper to him. Although he has no idea what I'm talking about at the ripe age of two, he grins brightly at my words. Picking him up, I reveal our presence in the doorway.

Tessa quickly stands, holding her round belly until she reaches us. Standing on her tiptoes, she wraps her arms around us both and laughs.

Quietly, she says, "It's a girl, but if you ever forget an appointment again. I'll be mad at you for a week."

Laughing, I squeeze my family tighter. "A week?"

Shrugging her shoulders, she giggles too. "And, I won't accept any letters. I can never resist a man who expresses his love through letters."

A small voice echoes through the room. "Kiss, Mommy," our son chants. "Yes, Mommy. A kiss, please," I tease before I place my mouth against hers.

The simple touch of her lips confirms for me love and romance will always exist for us.

Acknowledgements

I WOULD LIKE TO BEGIN with the two people whom will always be first in my life, **David** and **Sienna**. Dave, I'll never hold it against you that you haven't read my books because they just aren't your thing. I'll also never forget you told someone my books are like romance, but not really romance. Haha. I love you. Sienna, you can read my books in about five to ten years.

Trish Lyle and **Kristen Teshoney**, as usual, I will never be able to repay you for your support or friendship. Thank you for being honest and encouraging. There will never be enough "thank yous" to express my gratitude for pushing me to live my dream. I will be forever indebted to you both.

To my sister, my biggest fan, and my best friend, **Dawn Rickman**. I love you. There will never be a day that I don't thank God you were chosen to be my sister. You're the BEST older sister in the world! I love you.

Christine Kuttnauer, I'm so thankful for your eyes. I bet you've never heard that before, but seriously, you have the most amazing eyes. They see things most people don't catch. Also, your brain is pretty awesome, too. It has good thoughts and ideas. Oh, man and don't even get me started on your heart. It's so gigantic! It holds so much love and support for everyone you love. They all complete me.

Sara Ney, you save me when I think I might run screaming from the author life. You make me laugh. A lot. Your honesty, creative mind, and kind heart are an inspiration to me. I'm your desperado. Are you my Juliet? Because Ricky Martin.

Kristin Delcambre, your sweet and sincere care for my story and our friendship is one of the biggest blessings in my life. I'm lucky to call you friend. Thank you for Lenox. Thank you for being my friend.

Murphy Rae, there are so many things I could say to you, but they'll never be enough. I'll keep it simple, thanks for being you.

Book Swappers, you're everything to me.

Julie Titus, thank you for being so amazing. For understanding when I get inappropriate in text messages that I'm harmless. For your creative mind and the way, you devote yourself to your work. It's that devotion that gives me the most beautiful books.

To all of my friends and family who have taken the time to read my stories and who support me.

I want to thank the readers. Your kindness to me and your acceptance of my books into your "me" time is honestly so humbling and means everything to me. Thank you from my whole heart.

Last, but not least. Thank you to the REAL **Chad Borchgardt**. Although the recent years have separated us, you will always be one of my most cherished friends. I think of you every day. While, Tessa's Chad isn't exactly you, the heart of him is. The kindness, loyalty, humor, devotion and sassy mouth that made up Tessa's Chad are every bit the kind of friend you are to me. Maybe one day, Chad will be helping Tessa bury a body. I promise they won't get caught because orange doesn't look good on anyone. I love you!

About the Author

SHIRL RICKMAN IS A WRITER, a dreamer, and an optimist. A small town Texas girl currently residing in the San Francisco Bay Area, Shirl adores her husband, daughter, and two crazy dogs. When she's not dreaming up new love stories, Shirl can be found reading, drinking her favorite coffee, Kona Blend with coconut milk. She loves kindness, laughing and meeting her readers.

Website link:
https://shirl-rickman-author.squarespace.com/

Facebook:
https://www.facebook.com/shirlrickmanauthor/?pnref=story

Twitter:
https://twitter.com/shirl_rickman

Instagram:
https://www.instagram.com/shirlrickmanauthor/

Made in the USA
Columbia, SC
20 January 2022